Christmas Cracker Chaos

Jessica L. Jackson

Published by Bru E-books

The cover photograph was taken by Marina Willis

Original ISBN: 978-1-926467-22-1

Cover Art by Trifle Ink Design
trifleinkdesign@gmail.com

Bio:

Jessica L. Jackson lives with her English husband, one cat and two dogs in Southern Alberta, Canada. She has three children. She's been a member of the Alberta Romance Writers' Association for eight years and is a past-president. When not writing, she works as an Engineering Drafting Technician. Her favorite seasons are spring and fall. Jessica likes to camp, garden, cook, and listen to audiobooks while driving, working, doing the dishes, gardening, taking exercise and while waiting in the car for her family to come out of a store or their work.

She would like to acknowledge the continuing support of her family, whom she loves very much.

Jessica L. Jackson

Jessica L. Jackson

Introductory Prologue

Aunty stood in front of her frosty, diamond-paned window, staring out, and up, at the ribbons of purple, pink, and green light undulating across the dark night. Jeffrey, her red and black brindle guinea pig, chortled behind her from his post on the corner of the dining table.

"The aurora's singing loudly tonight, pet," she said. Though she frowned, her eyes danced with excitement. "They're singing it's time. It's time."

Aunty turned around and looked at Jeffrey. "Time for what, you ask? And well you might. It's been a good few years since I've made my special Christmas Crackers." Jeffrey sneezed. "Yes, before your time."

She scratched the side of her ample hip through the layers of woolen black bombazine and then reached out and smoothed Jeffrey's hair.

"I already have someone in mind for this year. A woman, I think. She is kind and loving. A school teacher," she added. Lifting her pet into her arms, she shuffled across the worn Persian carpet to the settle before the heat of the coal fire in the grate. She sat, stuffing cushions around her person and squirming until she felt comfortable.

"Hmm, who deserves her? And who does she deserve?"

Jeffrey purred.

"Yes, someone equally special," Aunty agreed. "He must be a hard worker. A peacemaker, I think, but valiant, too."

She fell silent, staring into the glowing fire as though she sorted through candidate after candidate. Jeffrey fell asleep against her deep bosom while the wind howled outside their cottage and the northern lights danced, singing to those who would listen and understand. Finally, the fire died down enough that Aunty bestirred herself. She stood, put Jeffrey in his bed on the floor in the corner, added a few more coals to the range in the kitchen, and took herself off to bed.

"Tomorrow," she mumbled tiredly, turning down the white eiderdown duvet and sheet, "I'll make a special Christmas cracker in my workroom and then take it to her."

Aunty, once ready for bed, climbed between the sheets and closed her eyes. *And, for next year? I think a man. Yes. A good man.*

The Christmas Cracker

Prologue

"Which one? Which one?"

An encouraging chortle answered her whispered questions.

Aunty closed her eyes and cocked her head to one side, concentrating on the impressions trickling through her fingertips as she stroked the ribbons and laces dangling from the dark wood rafters overhead. A length of curly ribbon caught at her thumb, wrapping around it so that when she moved, the ribbon came away into her hand.

"Ah," she sighed. "Iridescent magenta."

Aunty placed the ribbon on the worktable before she settled her cumbersome bulk onto the wooden stool before it. A wood fire sang in the grate on the far side of the cluttered room, warding off the snowy cold beyond the diamond-paned windows. A tray of colorful crackers filled one end of the wooden settle, their crepe paper ruffles gaily painted with sparkles. There were white ones, green ones, red ones and dark blue ones. Ordinary crackers with no special qualities—other than beauty. Aunty never made an ugly Christmas cracker.

Tiny baubles, beads, and silk flowers filled rows of painted terracotta pots marching across the short end of the table. Aunty dipped her hand into first one pot and then another.

"I need just the right…There, a heart-shaped bead and…and…yes…tiny silk roses."

She put the decorations with the length of satin ribbon. Everything she needed was now directly to hand. Her gnarled fingers hovered over the sheets of crepe paper hanging across dowels stuck into the wall beside the table. She touched first one color and then another, concentrating. A speculative gleam marked her sharp black eyes.

"Pink," she muttered, glancing at Jeffry, her red and black brindle guinea pig who sat placidly on the corner of the table. "Sally will be fascinated by a pink cracker." Her pet's ears twitched and he made no demure.

Aunty smoothed the crinkly paper out on the cold granite surface. She picked up a ruler and a pencil. Carefully, she drew the proper shaped rectangles on the sheet while murmuring a chant that popped out of her like air escaping bubbles on a millpond.

"A white tube goes well with pink…don't you think?" she asked, cackling brightly at her alliteration.

Jeffry emitted a long, loud squeal.

"Ah, lovely wheeking, Strong and powerful," Aunty commented, peering at Jeffry over the top of her half-moon spectacles. "So, you approve?"

He wheeked again.

"Excellent."

She rolled the crepe paper around the white tube and glued it in place. Next she prised a single paper doily, three inches in diameter, from a tightly layered stack of fifty others. A curse escaped her lips when she tore the first one. Jeffry's teeth chattered in agitation. She ignored him, and hissing joined the chattering.

"All right. All right," she grumbled, thrusting her hand into a leather sack purse sitting on a near-by stool. A shiny coin emerged, clutched between Auntie's thumb and forefinger. She pointed it at the guinea pig. "This was supposed to go inside Sally's cracker."

Jeffry purred.

"I'm so relieved that you're pleased with me," she snarled, dropping the coin onto the over-flowing swear jar. Several gold disks slipped from the pile and pinged off the counter. "Now, let me get back to work."

Jeffry tossed his head up into the air and turned partially away.

"Now you're in a snit," she complained, shaking her head. "Just sit still for a little while so I can finish Sally's cracker. You know it takes me a half hour to make each one." Jeffry chirped. "Thank you."

Aunty glued the white paper doily around the crepe-paper-wrapped tube. She held it close to her mouth and breathed the words across the lacy surface, infusing it with purpose. Setting the cracker down again, she picked up the length of curly ribbon and cut two smaller pieces from the whole.

"Beautiful," she murmured, letting the satin curl around her fingers. "You are for Sally."

Aunty glued the glowing ribbons around the tube, one at each end. Her chanting resumed. Sometimes, the words came in a breath of sound too low to be deciphered. At other moments, the chant roared through the room, rebounding off the white-washed walls before quenching itself inside the vibrating pink cylinder. When it came time to place the cardboard snapper inside the tube, she stroked the narrow strip between her fingers, keeping her eyes closed while she muttered promises of import.

"This Christmas cracker is for Sally," she pronounced. Jeffry popcorned into the air several times. His hair stood on end and he giggled. "That will be enough out of you," Aunty ordered, giving him a look. "This is an important step. Without the bang, this is no proper cracker." Jeffry stopped hopping up and down. "That's better."

Aunty held her breath as she eased the long thin snapper into the evolving cracker. One end fit through the hole in the middle of the gathered ruffle and the other hung out, waiting for the tube to be closed with another ruffle. First, it must be filled. Sally needed the prizes she'd find inside. The air in the small workroom crackled and fizzed with energy.

"Time to fill it."

The pile of surprises waited at her elbow. Aunty sung an ancient Christmas carol as she stuffed the four-inch by one inch tube with prizes, a motto, and a piece of salt-water taffy. She held up the final item and pointed it at Jeffry.

"I looked high and low for this," she said. "I couldn't buy it anywhere. I finally had to resort to dousing. The search wasn't easy, let me tell you. But, Sally has to have it."

Aunty stilled and the air in the room pulsed. Her unfocused eyes looked beyond the present. Out of the blue, she stated, her voice throbbing with meaning, *"She's the one for you, Jed. Don't let her go."*

The moment passed with a shake of her shoulders. Aunty pushed and shoved until she fit the final item into the tube. "Once I have this tied off…" She squeezed the pink crepe paper together at the open end around the snapper tail and fitted the second ruffle in place.

"There," she said, placing the cracker in the center of her worktable. "What do you think, Jeffry? Is it tempting enough? Is it beautiful enough?"

The guinea pig cooed.

Aunty was satisfied.

Chapter One

The Present

Sally waved goodbye to her last student as he trudged out into the cold December afternoon. They were going home to their families, to Christmas dinner, toys and candy. She envied them.

Sally fitted her purse, books and student gifts into her knapsack. She slipped it over her shoulders and stepped outside her classroom and into the hall. Sally looked down the deserted hallway and sighed. Fourteen days of Christmas holidays. Alone. She sighed again and pushed through the exit near her classroom.

She shuddered and leaned into the cold southern Alberta wind. She shoved her hands into her pockets and walked as quickly as possible across the school grounds to the ancient white church at the far corner of the playing fields. Recently restored, the church had been built over a hundred years before, right next to the old school that had long served as the church hall.

When she reached the church hall, she nodded to the rector who opened the door to let customers inside for the craft fair. She smiled in appreciation of the warmth and quickly shed her coat and placed it on a hook. She carried her knapsack over her arm and carefully moved through the crowded space, looking at the crafts presented on long rectory tables. Behind the tables sat women, and a few men, pointing out their handiwork's advantages.

Sally purchased a lovely fresh evergreen wreath entwined with red and gold velvet ribbons from the rector's wife. The money, she was assured, would go to buy toys for the less fortunate children in the parish. She paused at the bake table and bought a loaf of Christmas cake. She tucked that into her knapsack and turned to leave. But then she spotted a table beside the woodstove. Strange, but she hadn't noticed it when she'd circulated before.

She walked over and smiled at the rotund old woman sitting in a rocking chair behind a square table, upon which were laid a dozen Christmas crackers. The lady wore a colorful silk scarf over her brilliant white hair. Black Gypsy eyes twinkled merrily from behind half-moon gold spectacles. She waved a gnarled hand at her wares, smiling and crooning softly about the beauties laid out before her. The crackers were indeed lovely, in green, dark blue, red and white crêpe paper. The ruffles had been dusted with gold sparkles and tiny silk poinsettias had been arranged to decorate the five-inch cylinders.

"These are so beautiful," Sally exclaimed softly, reaching out to carefully touch one of the poinsettias. She raised her clear blue eyes to the vendor, who smiled benignly back at her.

"Those aren't for you, my dear," the old woman said in a raspy voice. Sally blinked in surprise. The old woman reached down under the table and pulled out a pastel-pink cracker and set it on the table before Sally. "I've been saving this beauty for someone special. Would you like to have it?"

Sally gazed at the cracker and sighed at its loveliness. A delicate white lace doily had been wrapped around the tube. Satin ribbons of pink adorned its the cylinder ends. Four tiny pink silk roses decorated the front. A red heart-shaped bead nestled among the roses, threaded through with a pink satin ribbon.

"Oh my," Sally breathed. She reached down and picked up the delicate-looking cracker and laid it across her palm. It felt surprisingly heavy. Eagerly, she asked, "How much?"

"It's a gift, my dear," the old woman demurred, shaking her white head at the schoolteacher.

"Oh, but…" Sally protested. However, her words were weak. She really wanted—no, *longed*—to have this Christmas cracker. The compulsion to own this confection in pink swept over her and it was with unreasonable relief that she heard the vendor's response to her objection.

"No, my dear. I made it for you. You deserve something extra special," she asserted, pulling her crocheted shawl more tightly about her. She reached beneath the table and drew out a white cardboard box just the right size to hold one cracker. "Put it in this so you won't crush it."

"Yes," Sally said, taking the box from the woman. She reverently placed the exquisite cracker inside the box. "Thank you so much. Merry Christmas," she said, smiling broadly at the woman.

The old woman nodded to her and Sally felt her eyes upon her as she walked away. "Pull it on Christmas morning, you hear?" she called out.

Sally nodded and smiled over her shoulder.

The old woman shook a finger at her. "Christmas morning."

* * * * *

Sally sat in the antique rocking chair before the fireplace in the front room, staring at the beautiful cracker resting in place of honor atop a lace tablecloth on a round cherrywood table across from her. She glanced at the grandfather clock standing tall and stately beside the entrance to the stairs leading to the two upstairs bedrooms. Two minutes to midnight.

Two minutes until I can pull the cracker. Sally licked her lips. She couldn't remember ever being this excited about the arrival of Christmas—certainly not since her parents had died when she was twelve.

Sally played with the long braid that hung over one shoulder. She twisted it this way and that, biting her lip. *I must wait. She said I had to wait until Christmas.* Sally stood and moved restlessly over to look out into the night. It was snowing again. Yesterday a blizzard had blown through, dropping ten inches of snow over the small town. By the look of things there was going to be another couple of inches by morning. *Christmas snow,* Sally thought with pleasure.

She dropped the dark-green velvet drapes back into place with a start as the grandfather clock began its resonant tolling of the twelfth hour. She raced across the carpet to stand before the table. She reached out a hand that trembled visibly in the candlelight. Only when the last toll had struck did Sally pick up the cracker.

She cradled it in her palms and sank to her knees on the rug before the fire. She took one end of the snapper in her left hand and the other in her right. She closed her eyes, made a Christmas wish and tugged. The resultant bang sounded louder than she would have expected, startling her.

She tugged the ruffle off one end and spilled the contents into the lap of her white flannelette nightgown. She poked through the hoard.

"How did all this fit inside?" she wondered aloud. "That explains its weight."

She picked up the hat and unfolded it. Instead of a crown, the pink tissue hat turned out to be a poke bonnet. She laughed with delight and placed it on her head. She tied the tissue ribbons carefully so as not to tear them. The next item to catch her eye was a wax-paper-wrapped candy. She untwisted it and discovered a pull of saltwater taffy. She poked it into her mouth and sucked on it until it was soft enough to chew. Delicious.

Her next choice was a folded cloth. She was pleased to hold in her hand a white lace handkerchief. Embroidered in one corner were her initials, S.W.

Now, how could she have known...? Sally looked up into the crackling fire.

She shook her head and returned to picking through her prizes. She puzzled over the ancient key, wondering why the old woman had put it inside the cracker. A small fawn purse, roughly the size of her fist, opened with a drawstring. Sally poured the contents onto her skirt. Shiny silver and copper coins spilled out. She lifted one and tilted it to catch the

14

firelight.

"1899," she murmured, a touch of awe entering her voice

She counted out twenty-five dollars in coinage. She shook her head, amazed, then replaced the money inside the purse. Logically, the money had come from the cracker, but there was no way she could fit the purse back inside the cylinder. Sally paused to pick the taffy from her teeth before putting the prizes on the floor beside her. Only after she had placed them all in a row did she spot the bone toggle button resting in the folds of her nightgown. It was three inches long and she couldn't understand how she missed seeing it before. Among all the rest, a small slip of paper fluttered.

The motto. Sally smoothed out the strip and read the saying out loud.

"'If we open a quarrel between the past and the present, we shall find we have lost the future.'" She arched her eyebrows. "Winston Churchill." She put the motto with the rest of her loot.

As impossible as it seemed, all the prizes had come from the cracker, but Sally had no idea how. When the old woman had said the cracker was unusual, Sally hadn't thought she meant that it was bigger on the inside than it appeared on the outside! A veritable Tardis in fact.

"Well, Merry Christmas to me," Sally murmured, smiling widely and shaking her head in amazement. She gathered her prizes and deposited them on the cherrywood table. She added the opened cracker to the pile.

She banked the wood fire before blowing out the candles and making her way to her room in the dark.

Her farmhouse had been built more than an hundred years before of brick—the same brick that had been used to build the irrigation canals. Thick, smooth plaster covered the inside walls. There was a large front room, directly off the entrance, a large eat-in kitchen the same size as the front room, a half bath under the stairway, a main bedroom off the front room, and two bedrooms tucked under the eaves on the upper floor. The full-sized bathroom had been added only forty-five years before. It had been built at one end of the enclosed porch off the back entrance so that Sally had to go through the porch to get to the bathroom to take a bath in the mornings. She tried to keep the back porch warm but it was still chilly in the depths of winter.

Sally loved the old house. Her parents had purchased it twenty-three years before, when she was six, and had restored it so it looked much as it had when originally built—except for the bathrooms, of course. She had added to their antiques collection, purchasing the iron bedstead she used from a woman downtown whose store specialized in early District of Alberta furniture.

Sally remembered the tissue poke bonnet only after she put her head on her pillow. She chuckled to herself and removed it, setting it on one of the bed knobs. She pulled the tied crazy quilt up over her slender frame and snuggled down, willing the cold sheets to warm up. She sighed, strangely content for the first Christmas in many years.

Chapter Two

Christmas morning, 1899

"Whoa," Jed called, pulling back on the reins.

The two black horses obediently stopped and snorted clouds of hot breath through their wide nostrils. Jed wrapped the reins around the sled's brake handle before climbing down from the wooden seat. His wolf-hide and fur boots were laced around the calves to keep them up. He wore buckskins under the bear fur poncho that hung down to his knees. Thick fur mittens protected his hands.

The new snow crunched and squeaked under Jed's feet as he moved around to the back of the sleigh. He tugged on the handle of a heavy trunk and dragged it over to him. He turned around and pulled it up onto his broad shoulders. He grunted and leaned over under its weight, then trudged to the front porch of the new house. Jed stared for a moment at the wreath hanging on the panel door, then he lowered the trunk onto the porch floor. He raised his fist and knocked loudly.

Sally rolled over under the quilt and groaned. Was that the door? The pounding came again. It sounded like an elephant. She reluctantly threw off her covers and gasped at the cold, tempted to retreat back into the warmth of her bed. *Good thing I have a woodstove in the kitchen and a fireplace in the front room,* she thought, *because the furnace must be on the blink.* The knock came again. She hastily yanked on her robe and shoved her feet into slippers and rushed out of her bedroom.

"I'm coming, I'm coming," she called, rubbing the sleep from her eyes with the heel of her hand. When she reached the door she paused and said, "Who is it?"

"Preacher. I've brought your trunk."

The muffled words did not explain much to her and she didn't know any "Preacher".

"I can leave it out here if you want, ma'am, but it's awful heavy and you mightn't be able to manage it."

"Ma'am?" Sally murmured, perplexed. *What the heck?* She cautiously opened the door and peered out. A bear of a man stood on her front porch and he did indeed have a very large sturdy trunk standing upright beside him. He nodded to her, hefted the trunk and pushed through the door before she could repudiate him. She gave a little yelp of surprise and jumped back out of the way.

"Mornin'. Sorry to have gotten you out of bed, ma'am," he said, looking around for a place to set the trunk. "How 'bout I set it here, by the wall?" And he did just that.

"But…" Sally managed to get out before the frigid morning air swirled around the door, distracting her. She pushed the door shut and turned to face the delivery man. It looked like he was wearing a bearskin poncho, for heaven's sake! *A throwback to the mountain men of the 1800s, if ever there was one,* she thought, amused. He appeared to be a little older than herself but it was hard to tell. "That can't be my trunk."

"It's the only trunk from last night's train that's come down from Lethbridge," he explained reasonably.

He tugged off his beaver skin hat with its earflaps and held it between his mittened hands, revealing black curly hair that seemed to run straight into sideburns and then into a huge bushy dark brown beard. His chestnut-brown eyes pierced hers in a disconcerting manner, as if he were sizing her up. But for what? Sally was afraid to ask. Not afraid as in a "he's going to throw me down and rape me" sort of fear, but the sort of fear that came when you didn't think you'd like the answer.

"The crates of school primers and things arrived yesterday too. I've put them in the schoolhouse for you. I see you've set your furniture about nicely already." He frowned over her continued confusion and pointed to the large brass plate mounted above the trunk's lock. "Those are your initials, aren't they ma'am? S. W. for Sally Winters?" He pointed to the big iron key sitting on the doily on the table. "That's the key for it, isn't it?"

"Um," Sally said, turning wide eyes from him to the key nestled among the cracker paraphernalia. It couldn't be, could it? She took a step toward the table, then another, feeling as though she was wading through a dream. The delivery man stood out of the way for her. She picked up the key, held it tightly between her two fisted hands and approached the trunk.

"Here, let me set that down properly for you," the man said, tilting the trunk so it sat four-square on the floor.

"Thank you," she murmured automatically as she sank to her knees before the chest. Her hands trembled a bit as she fitted the big key to the brass lock. Holding her breath, she turned it. The tumblers clicked open.

"I'd best be off, then," he was saying. "I'll come back later to see if you'll be wantin' anythin'. Merry Christmas."

"Um, yes. Merry Christmas," Sally replied absently, lifting the heavy lid. His words sank in, finally, and she turned frowning eyes on him. "What was that?" But he was gone and she could hear horses outside being told to "giddy up". Horses? Why would he need to come back? Not that she objected, precisely, for he'd been a rather fascinating individual, but why would a delivery man think that she'd want anything from him? And another thing—since when did trains stop anywhere in Southern Alberta these days just to drop off a trunk? On Christmas Eve, no less. Maybe he meant the bus. That made more sense.

Sally shrugged her confusion aside in the pleasure of looking through *her* trunk. *It can't really be my trunk,* she thought, but then wriggled with excitement. *It's my key. It's my initials. It must be mine—however improbable that it should be so, it must be mine.* A shiver ran through her and she realized she could see her breath in the cold air. Looking longingly at the prizes she glimpsed inside the trunk, she decided she'd enjoy them more if she wasn't freezing cold.

Jed sat for a moment on the bench of his sleigh, the reins slack in his hands. The new schoolteacher was mighty comely. That blonde hair, the color of ripened wheat, those blue eyes, wide and staring, those full lips, that pretty, freckled nose, all added up to one acceptable package. Very acceptable, he admitted, frowning heavily over that. He hadn't expected to be attracted to her himself. He'd never found white women all that attractive. They seemed pasty compared to the darker skin of his Kainai cousins.

A half-breed himself, he often wished he looked more like his mother. Many who had known his black-haired French Canadian father thought that he favoured him entirely—thus the curly hair and full beard. The Catholic priests had tried to force the Kainai out of him, so he'd learned to speak like the English-speaking settlers. The Mormon elders had been much nicer but he'd not been tempted over to their religion. Instead he'd formed his own thoughts and beliefs and shared them where he would, to the annoyance of the Catholic priests and the amusement of the Mormon ones, which was why they called him Preacher.

Looking more like a white man had certain advantages, he could not deny. However, when it came time for the new teacher to choose a husband, he doubted it would be him. The interested single men had been gathering in Crombly over the last week.

Come the day after tomorrow, Miss Winters, along with the two other single ladies who had come down especially from Lethbridge, will have a goodly number to choose from.

Just yesterday he'd seen Jeremy Woodruff from the new village of Stirling staying at the boarding house. Three others had ridden over from Fort MacLeod and two rascals had come down on the train from Fort Kipp. He hoped she wouldn't pick one of them. The town didn't need one of those types living in it.

A rancher who had a spread down Buffalo Flats way was expected in the morning. Here in Crombly, the widower doctor had implied that he might throw his hat in. The blacksmith, also a widower but with five children to look after, was in dire need of a wife as his youngest was only six months old. However, Miss Winters had to teach school, too, so how she was to look after a houseful of young children Jed didn't know. If he counted up all those interested that he knew of, there were surely twenty men at least who would be there to look the women over. He wouldn't be there to choose, though he'd agreed to be there as a witness. She was too white and he was not white enough.

Jed called "Giddy up," to his draft horses and pulled away from the nice new house with its pretty new resident.

Chapter Three

Sally stared at the tin bucket, brim full of black coal, and blinked twice. She turned her gaze to the fancy new range that looked nothing like the woodstove her grandmother had used for seventy years—they'd moved it into this house when her parents had died and Gran had come to look after her. The gleaming name plate read "The Regal". Feeling somewhat as if she were having an out-of-body experience, Sally slowly looked this way and that, noting other changes to her kitchen. It *was* her kitchen, but it also *wasn't* her kitchen. Instead of being embroidered with cherries, the white curtains had blue gingham ruffles. Instead of an old dark brown dresser parked beneath a daisy clock, used to hold linen, now there was a pine Hoosier cabinet. No electric clock graced the wall above. The kitchen sink seemed like the same one, but now there were no black nicks to mar the white porcelain.

The floor was finished with dark red linoleum, gleaming with new wax. Hers had been replaced five years before with a mottled pale turquoise faux marble linoleum—one the manufacturer had assured her was similar to a pattern they had produced in the twenties. The 1920s, that is. A large woven rag rug sat beneath her kitchen table, or rather beneath one that was almost the same as her kitchen table. But this rug's pattern and color differed from her own. In the centre of the ceiling the glass light fixture that also hailed from the twenties had been replaced with a kerosene lamp.

"This can't be right," Sally whispered, opening her eyes wide. "What is going on?"

A sudden horrible thought crossed her mind and she rushed to the back door. *Please God.* "Please God," she prayed beneath her breath. She unlocked the door and yanked it open, revealing her back porch. Still not satisfied, Sally stumbled out into the cold, enclosed space and looked to her left.

She really felt like swearing. Swearing really, really hard. However, she'd trained herself not to curse so that she'd never accidentally let something slip in class. Besides, her Gran had disapproved. But now she had to ferociously bite back at least half a dozen really, really good ones.

The bathroom was gone. Where it had once been a huge open wooden box stood filled with coal. A shovel leaned against the waist-high container, mocking her. Sally started breathing heavily, feeling as if she might hyperventilate. A copper hip tub—the old-fashioned kind, bright and new—hung from a large nail right next to the back door.

The cold struck her bladder and she whimpered, for through the glass in the back door she had just spotted the dreaded outhouse. It had a cut-out of an apple in the door. Clever.

"This is not happening to me!" she cried softly.

Sally looked at the new snow lying on the ground between her and her salvation and started to look around for a pair of boots. There were none on the porch. She hurried back into the house and her eyes lighted on the trunk. Quickly, she started to make piles of its contents. She formed piles of cotton and wool undergarments, socks, blouses and skirts. A large dark blue woollen shawl she placed around her shivering body. At the bottom of the trunk she found a sturdy pair of black leather granny boots—at least that was what she used to call them when she was a little girl.

Hastily she tugged on a pair of wool socks, fitted her feet into the boots—sparing no thought as to why they fit perfectly—grabbed a pair of mittens and a woollen toque from a pile, then raced out the two back doors and made a path to the necessary, where she found that someone had obligingly supplied her with a tin containing Albany Medicated toilet paper.

"Darn, it's cold," she gasped.

Any thought that she might be dreaming froze the moment

she sat down on the cold toilet seat. However improbable…however impossible…she'd gone back in time—a good hundred years or so, she figured. It was madness. It was lunacy. But here she was, shivering in antiquated facilities, behind a house that was hers but not quite hers. How would she cope? Could she get back to her own time, since she didn't know how she'd got here to begin with?

An image of the little old cracker lady flashed into her mind. "Oh, if I ever get my hands on you…"

* * * * *

Sally felt the numbing cold settle into her bones and wrap tendrils around her brain as she stared, unseeing, at the coal piled in the grate. An open box of matches rested on her slack palm.

1899.

Wow.

1899.

Wow.

Her thoughts couldn't seem to move beyond this repeating madness.

1899.

Impossible.

Clearly not.

1899.

Impossible.

Clearly not *impossible,* Sally amended. Her growling stomach drew her out of her reverie and she struck another match. It flared and she placed it under the edge of a piece of coal. Why had she never listened when Gran had told her stories of using coal before the local seams had run out? She dropped the charred match stump onto the hearth among its stubborn cohorts. Not a whiff of smoke could be seen among the coal.

"If Preacher doesn't return," she muttered, rising stiffly to her feet, "I'm going to freeze to death in my own home."

Sally moved to the window, hugging her shawl around her. She gazed wistfully out at the smoke puffing merrily from her neighbors' chimneys. Alternatively, she'd have to embarrass herself by asking for help from a neighbor. Who knew how much she might reveal with her ignorance?

Her growling stomach drove her to look in the Hoosier and the cupboards for something to eat that wasn't frozen and didn't need cooking. There she found some crackers and a crock of honey. While munching on these comestibles, Sally remembered that there had originally been a root cellar beneath the back porch. Further investigation proved her memory correct. She lifted the floor hatch and peered down into the dark. She lit the lantern hanging on a nail by the back door and carefully climbed down into the hole.

In the large root cellar she discovered rows of home-canned goods—not frozen, thank goodness—and barrels of apples, carrots in sand, and sacks of potatoes, onions and beets. A lovely jumble of cabbages sat beside a pile of turnips and a compilation of different squashes. A ham hung from one corner among about a dozen smoked sausage rings. A truly massive slab of bacon and a goodly collection of beef jerky rounded off the stored meat. Eggs nestled in a basket of straw on a rough plank shelf. A crock of butter and a pitcher of milk also sat there along with a large wheel of hard cheese. *It was a hoard of food*, Sally thought, much relieved. She drank thirstily from the milk jug before grabbing an apple and retreating to her bedroom.

Once beneath the covers and munching on the crisp, cold apple, she rehearsed what she could say to her neighbors that wouldn't make her seem like an imbecile. Maybe she could lure a passing child into the house and get her to "teach" the new teacher how to light a coal fire. *And how long would it take for her ignorance to spread around this small town?* Sally harrumphed, sneaking her hand out into the cold air to place the apple core on her bedside table.

Probably not one of my better ideas, Sally thought fuzzily, feeling her eyelids droop. *Shock,* she mused. *Must be. The way to light the coal is likely to be so obvious that I'm going to feel stupid no matter what.*

Chapter Four

True to his word, Jed returned to the teacher's house later that afternoon to see how she was. The lack of smoke coming out of the chimneys concerned him so when she didn't answer his pounding knock, he cautiously opened the door.

"Miss Winters?" Jed saw the remnants of considerable effort to start the fire in the front room. There were numerous matches littering the pile of coals in the grate but no burnt paper or kindling or bundles of dried grass to show that she'd begun the fire correctly.

Jed closed the front door and called out again. He barely heard an, "I'm in here," from the back bedroom.

"I'll start your fire for you," he called.

"Yes please," she called in a muffled voice.

Jed shook his head. *She must be huddled under the covers.* He went out onto the back porch and returned with four bundles of knotted dried grass and an armload of kindling. He took off his fur mittens, removed the coal piled in the grate and began to lay the fire, putting two bundles of dried grass on the bottom, then some kindling to catch fire from the grass, then a handful of coal bits on top of those, then some larger pieces on top of the small ones. The door to the bedroom opened just as he was about to strike a match. The teacher rushed out, a thick shawl wrapped about her head and a quilt wrapped around her shoulders. She looked pale, as if she'd had a jolt.

"I'd better learn how to do it right," she said, hunkering down beside him. She looked up at him and gave him a wavering smile. "I got so cold I went back to bed. I'm so glad you returned. I've never used coal before."

"I suspicioned as much." Jed captured the perfume of roses about her in a big breath and didn't want to let it go. He exhaled, finally, and felt a flush rising at her continued earnest regard.

"What did you say your name was?"

"People call me Preacher."

"But, that's not your real name, surely?"

Jed pressed his lips together. *She might as well know now as later.* "Jedidiah Pierre Runs-With-the-Wind Lavine."

"Your father was a French Canadian?" Miss Winters asked, then waved rather urgently toward the coals.

Jed put the match to a bundle of grass, which immediately caught. "Yes, but he wasn't Catholic. He was Jewish."

"Hmm," was all she said. Then, "Your mother? Is she of the people?" she asked in the Blackfoot tongue. Jed dropped the box of matches and reared up to tower over her. She fell back onto her bottom and glared at him. "Is my accent that bad?"

"I am surprised, is all." Jed backed away a step, swept up the other two grass bundles, the remaining kindling and the box of matches, then stalked into the kitchen.

"So, is she Kainai?" Sally asked, rising to chase after him. He grunted, so she took that as yes. "I've never cooked on a stove like this," she admitted, watching him set about laying a fire in the fire box. "I've cooked on a woodstove, of course," she boasted.

"Of course."

"No, really, I have," Sally promised. "There are more dampers on this than I'm used to. I'll get the hang of it." She pulled the quilt more tightly around her. "As soon as I figure out how to light the beast."

"There are more of these grass knots and a pile of kindlin' on the back porch. Once the fire is well lit it's best not to let it go out. Particularly in winter. If you're tempted to stir the coals like a wood fire, resist."

"I will. I saw the kindling and grass knots earlier but I just couldn't seem to think clearly."

Jed frowned and stared at her hard. His dark brown eyes

appeared almost black and when she stared into them they seemed fathomless. "School starts in eight days, Miss Winters. You'd best be settled in and thinkin' clearly by then," he warned.

Beneath her breath, Sally murmured, "I was right. I'm still a teacher."

"What was that?"

"Hmm? Nothing. Nothing."

Jed looked askance but just said, "I've some questions I need to ask you afore I leave. They are for the introductions at the meetin' the day after tomorrow."

"Meeting?"

"Yes, the meetin' where you choose a husband. It's in your contract. As part of the terms you're promised a husband."

"Come again?" Sally gasped. "Promised a husband?"

"Yes," Jed said slowly, puzzled by her shock. He sighed and hooked his thumbs into the wide belt enclosing his bear-fur poncho. "You and two other spinsters have been promised husbands. There will be at least twenty to choose from. Quite a variety."

"Spinsters? Huh. And how is this supposed to work, exactly?" she demanded, stomping over to the kitchen table. She took a chair and carried it over beside the stove. "Go ahead—grab a chair and sit down. I've got a few questions for you too."

Jed brought a chair over to face her but before he sat down he unbuckled his belt and removed his bear skin poncho, revealing a thick red wool coat. He opened the toggles on the coat before he sat down.

"One of your toggles is missing. Just a sec," she said, jumping up from her chair. "I think…"

Jed watched her move off into the front room, search through some items on the small table by the fire and return with her fist clenched around something. She stopped in front of him and held open her hand. His missing toggle—or one remarkably like it—lay on her flat palm.

"Son of a gun," he said, reaching for the bone toggle. He compared it with his own, but while his were white, this one had yellowed with age. Otherwise they appeared identical. "How?"

"No idea."

"Strange."

"Yes it is."

Jed rose to tend the fire, pocketing the button. After he saw that the fire was in a fair way, he opened the tin breadbox on the counter and saw that the loaf of bread there hadn't been touched. He took the frozen bread over to the stove, placed it in the warming oven and turned back to sit.

"So, what's this about my being a spinster and getting a husband?" Sally asked, watching Jed sit back down. "I'm only twenty-nine, you know." He stroked his full beard and eyed her reflectively.

"Well?"

Jed scowled at her urgency. "As I said afore, your contract with the town includes, besides this house and your wage, the choice of a husband."

"Then I don't have to choose one if I don't wish to?" she pressed.

"The board will not like that. They promised you a husband. You have the choice of who to marry, but not *if* you marry."

"How quickly would the wedding take place?" Sally asked, panic sparking in her eyes. She threw off the quilt and drew the shawl down around her shoulders. Her soft golden-blonde hair was mussed and her braid had loosened, letting wisps of fine hair fall down around her face.

"Immediately," Jed said. "There will be a preacher there. Reverend Lammers, I believe." He watched her rise and pace. Her brown woollen skirt swished around her ankles as she moved. Her agitation was readily apparent. "Why did you agree to the terms if you disliked them?"

Sally seemed to be chewing on an agitated retort but her

reply when it came was mild and confusing.

"My hand was forced."

"By who?"

"Whom," she instructed, beginning to wring her hands.

Jed sighed. "By *whom*?" He reached for her as she came close to him in her pacing. His hand closed about her hands and he tugged her over. "Please. Sit."

Jed kept hold of her cold wringing hands as he pushed her back into her chair. He liked the feel of her soft skin. He leaned forward and enclosed her hands in his large warm ones. Suddenly she leaned forward, too, and pressed her lips to his. The kiss startled him so much that before he could respond she'd pulled away.

"Why did you do that?" he asked, keeping his tone reasonable though his heart had skipped a beat and was now thudding alarmingly. Her fair cheeks flushed red and she looked away shyly.

"Bold, wasn't it?" She laughed softly but he thought the sound seemed a mite frantic. "I wanted to know what it would be like to kiss a stranger. If…if I marry a stranger, I'll have to do more than kiss him, won't I? How is that going to be? Well? *Well?* Maybe for men it's nothing," she cried softly, shrugging her shoulders and taking heaving breaths. "Maybe for the men it will be as nothing…marrying and bedding a complete stranger. How? How am I to bear it?" She turned searching eyes to his and Jed realized she required an answer.

"I don't know. I've never married and I've never bedded a stranger."

Jed's simple answer gave Sally no comfort. However, it did give her some more information about him—more information than she had about any of the other single men from whom she was supposed to choose. She had liked the kiss too. His beard tickled. His warm hands still held hers in a comforting grip that she also found oddly sensual. While she answered his questions about her talents and skills almost automatically, she was thinking feverishly.

"Enough questions," Sally said at last, her stomach growling again. She pulled her hands from Jed's and took off her shawl. She folded it, placed it on the chair and replaced the chair at the table. The discarded quilt joined the shawl. Returning to his side, she set her hand on his shoulder, indicating that he needn't rise.

"I've got to eat something. I've only had crackers and an apple all day. Would you like some bread? I could make toast? I saw some preserves in the Hoosier earlier. It's not much of a Christmas dinner, but I could try to put something together later. Unless you have somewhere you need to be?"

Unaccountably, he felt her touch through his coat, his shirt, and his long johns. He felt as if he'd been branded. The feeling grew in him until it reached down into his very soul. The restlessness that lived in those deep recesses stilled for a moment and took notice. He turned his head, looked into her blue eyes, and read resolve there. He jerked to his feet. Her hand trailed down his sleeve, tracing radiant fire on his skin beneath.

"I almost forgot to tell you. We are both invited to the mayor's house for Christmas dinner."

"Ah," she murmured, frowning. "Where does the mayor live?"

"I'll be round to collect you at about five o'clock," he stated clearly, though his mind felt as if it were filled with buzzing insects. "I'll go now," he said, acting like a hare ready to bolt before the coyote's howl. He moved quickly out of the kitchen and through to the front room.

When he turned to say good-bye, he found her on his heels, smiling brightly at him. She had beautiful, white, even teeth. He'd never seen teeth so brilliant. Or hair so golden and glowing. Or smelled a scent so sweet that the wild roses were put to shame. Or seen a figure so slight and becoming—like a willow, strong and supple. Before he could stop himself, he leaned down and captured her lips with his own. They were as soft and yielding as he had imagined. As tender as fresh sweet grass in the spring. As delicious as wild honey.

Sally drowned beneath the pleasure his lips brought her. Kissing an almost-stranger stole the strength from her limbs and turned her insides to jelly. When he slanted his lips over hers, she leaned further into the kiss and parted her lips. As she hoped, his tongue touched hers. Tentatively, she tasted him and he tasted wonderful. She reached up and let her fingers curl through his ticklish beard. A shudder passed through her.

He broke off the kiss far too soon for her liking and she sighed against his lips. In an instant he was gone, leaving her standing before the closed front door, a yearning in her being that she'd never felt before.

Sally turned around and leaned against the rough planks. She raised trembling fingers to her softened lips. *Could this Christmas bring me the love that I've been missing in my life? Maybe if that cracker lady appears, now,* she thought with a mischievous grin playing over lips recently kissed so soundly, *I'll give the old dear a hug, instead of a scold.*

Chapter Five

"Ah, here we are," Sally murmured, recognizing their destination.

Mayor Carmichael's house looked much as it had in her time, except it looked almost as new as her home. It had a wide Victorian-style white porch attached to the front of a large brick house. Evergreen garlands and crimson ribbons festooned the tops of the tall windows and the length of the porch rails. Two small cottonwood trees had been planted on either side of the wide brick walkway. In her time the massive trees shaded the entire house and the front concrete sidewalk.

"What a beautiful home," she said, looking from the house to Jed to judge his reaction, but he'd likely seen the structure many times before. His face showed no expression. *Does he get the ability to look like a stone from his mother's family,* she mused, refusing to let her mood be affected by his sober mien. "I've always preferred brick buildings."

And still, he said nothing in response to her comments. Sally doubted he'd ever be loquacious—yet, he must be able to expound on some subjects or else he'd never have earned the nickname 'Preacher'. Perhaps, it was her presence that had struck him dumb. What a pleasant thought.

Jed pulled up his horses and tied off the reins before turning to help Miss Winters down from the sleigh. She grinned widely at him but he kept his face impassive. She looked as pretty as a picture this evening with her hair pinned up and the cold lending her cheeks a becoming pink glow and her lips a rosy tinge, ready to be kissed again. For the remainder of the afternoon all he had thought about was the kiss they had shared. Not the first, surprise kiss, but the hungry

34

second one. He wondered if she remembered the kiss too, and when her eyes twinkled up at his he knew that she did.

They had not spoken much on the drive over. Other than a gruff "good evening", he'd sat silent beside her as she twisted this way and that, exclaiming softly beneath her breath. Sometimes it had sounded as if she were saying things like, "Oh, that's still the same." Or, "I don't remember that house being there." But she'd spoken so quietly that he couldn't be sure. The comments didn't make sense. Miss Winters had never been to Crombly.

Their host opened the door himself, welcoming them effusively into his home. His was a florid, plump countenance. His bald head gleamed in the lamplight and his fleshy mouth beamed.

"Come in. Come in," he cried, bustling them out of the cold. "Merry Christmas to you both. Preacher," he said, nodding genially. "And you must be Miss Winters, our new teacher?"

"Yes I am. Merry Christmas," Sally said, permitting Jed to remove her heavy wool coat, exposing a crisp white blouse with full leg-o'-mutton sleeves. A fancy light blue knitted vest covered the bodice of the blouse and the blouse had been tucked into a pleated navy skirt. She held out her hand. "Mayor Carmichael?"

"Yes, yes. That's my name." The Mayor laughed. He pulled an extremely thin, handsome woman of about fiftyish over. "This is my rib, Cora. My luv, this is Miss Winters."

"My dear, do come out of the foyer. You must be frozen after your drive over. No doubt Preacher has taken good care of you but we mustn't have you catching your death before school starts, must we?"

Sally tried to demur that she wasn't cold but the woman kept on and on about this subject and that while she introduced her to their other guests, who consisted of the Presbyterian minister and his wife Reverend and Mrs. Lammers, the local Doctor, a widower, and also a solicitor and his wife, Mr. and

Mrs. Busbee. Before long Sally had the histories of each member of their group—including her own. Apparently, she was supposed to have come from back east in the Toronto area. She was supposed to be an orphan—thank goodness there wouldn't be any family showing up whom she should recognize. Also, she was considered a prize teacher whom everyone was happy to have captured. Cora Carmichael was a woman who knew everything about everyone and liberally shared that information.

Everyone was very jolly over the Christmas goose, roast potatoes, cabbage rolls, mashed turnips and glazed carrots. Sally had been seated next to the Doctor and across the table from Preacher. Knowing he was half Kanai, she was impressed with how easily he blended into this gathering. She overheard him discussing the establishment of a lending library with the solicitor's wife, who whole-heartedly agreed with the project and had offered the use of one of their outbuildings—a sound, dry building that contained a coal stove and even a window.

"Perhaps Miss Winters would join me on a trip to Lethbridge to see what books we might obtain for the library?" Mrs. Busbee suggested, smiling across the table at Sally. "There is an admirable new-and-used book store there."

"I would be delighted," Sally agreed, nodding thoughtfully. "I need to review the primers and supplies, first, to be certain the school has everything it needs. I certainly wish to have a nice collection of children's books for the school's library."

"I have a copy of *Treasure Island* and I believe I have a copy of *The Jungle Book,* as well," Doctor Wright interjected. Tall, balding and slender, he had a naturally sour face, but his manner proved to be amiable and intelligent. "I would be happy to donate them to either library."

"That is excellent!" Mrs. Busbee praised, clapping her hands together in delight.

The others joined in with promises of books from their own precious collections. Sally felt flushed with excitement and anticipation for her new and most unexpected post.

Jed tried to ignore how pretty Miss Winters looked with her glowing eyes and soft pale skin radiant in the candlelight. As she eagerly discussed plans for the school and the number of pupils she'd be teaching Jed noticed the knowing glances exchanged between the married couples. They thought, he expected, that the doctor, though just over forty, was in a fair way to being smitten.

Jed doubted that it ever occurred to them that he might be feeling the same way. Everyone assumed that when he married it would be to a Kanai woman for he had never shown any interest in single white ladies. The teacher, they probably thought, was a well-cultured woman who would likely prefer a cultured man, like the doctor. They all took for granted Jed's ability to hold his own in their conversations for they never gave it a thought. If ever it crossed their minds they likely attributed his manners and knowledge to the Catholic priests who'd taught him.

"Miss Winters?" Reverend Lammers, a large, bullish Dutchman of indeterminate age, leaned around his wife to address Sally. She turned and smiled at him. "May I ask which religion do you belong to? Dare I hope that you count yourself as a Presbyterian?"

Sally stared owlishly at him for a moment, wondering what to say.

"Well, we know she's not a Mormon because we specifically advertised for a teacher who was *not* a Mormon," Mayor Carmichael stated emphatically, wagging his thick eyebrows. "More and more of those people are immigrating into this area from below the border and before we know it there will be more of them than there are of us."

"You are correct. I am not a Mormon," Sally supplied, frowning now. *What difference does it make what religion I profess?*

"But, you are a good, Christian woman—I can tell,"

Doctor Robbins inserted, smiling broadly at her and then at everyone else.

Sally nodded automatically, because she had always considered herself a Christian. She looked at Preacher, who sat stone-faced across from her. His eyes burned into hers, however, and it was with great difficulty that she managed to pull her gaze away.

"Toronto is a cosmopolitan city, no doubt, with people of many different religions living within its limits," Mr. Busbee noted. He gave her a sympathetic look. "Miss Winters, I am sure, has not considered the religious demographics of our small community. Have you, ma'am?"

"I confess that my students' religious beliefs have not concerned me in the past," Sally said slowly, setting down her fork and resting her hands on her lap. "I have always encouraged acceptance of the individual, regardless of his race, creed or religion. Surely, at this Christmas season, we understand that we must all live in harmony together, do we not?"

"Agreed."

Preacher's stark, simple answer drew everyone's attention. They remained silent for a moment and then they all began to hum and haw and sputter as they remembered his mixed heritage.

"We just feel," the Reverend Lammers rushed out, fidgeting with his spoon, turning it around and around on the white tablecloth, "that like fits better with like. At the meeting the day after tomorrow, you will be choosing a husband, as will the two other spinsters who arrive tomorrow, and we on the council have agreed that everyone's religious affiliations should be revealed at the outset so that there are no surprises after the weddings."

"You realize, I am certain," Mrs. Lammers continued when her husband's explanation had been met with a blank stare from Sally, "that in circumstances like this, the more a couple know about each other, the better their choice will be?"

"Of course," Sally murmured automatically. In the

enjoyment of the evening she had almost managed to forget that she was supposed to pick a complete stranger to marry. Though momentarily surprised by this preoccupation with religion, she accepted that she should have realized how historically important it was. Community life revolved around the local church congregations. "I was raised Church of England."

"There, then, that's settled," Mrs. Carmichael gushed. "Let's have some pumpkin pie. Or, we've got some lovely mincemeat tarts. Would anyone like some custard on their dessert?"

"Yes please," came from all quarters.

* * * * *

Sally allowed Jed to tuck the fur rug about her legs before he climbed into the sled. The brilliant moon shone down on the new snow, giving them plenty of light to drive by. The party had lasted until almost midnight and they had left a few of their fellow guests still lolling on the sofas in the parlor.

"I enjoyed myself very much," Sally murmured, boldly taking Jed's arm as he negotiated a turn onto her street. He stiffened but did not shake her off. She peered up at him. "Did you? I thought the talk around the table might have offended you."

"I choose not to be offended," Jed replied, shrugging. "They do not always think before they speak and, like the other town folk, they often forget that I am not white."

They pulled up in front of her house and sat for a moment. Jed looked at her. And looked some more. Sally sat still and returned his regard, waiting for him to speak. The moon cast his face mostly in shadow and she strained to see into his eyes. Still he did not speak. A coyote barked in the distance, breaking his stare. He looked to the foothills, then quickly climbed out and reached to lift her down to the snowy road.

"Thank you. Merry Christmas," Sally said, grinning up at him, her voice strangely airless. Her crystalline breath swirled between them. His stillness felt mysterious and exhilarating. "Will you be coming around to see me tomorrow? In the morning? I'd like to see the schoolhouse but I don't have the keys."

"I have the keys. I will bring them tomorrow afternoon," Jed finally spoke, his voice deep and resonant. "In the morning I am attending a sweat lodge."

"I thought sweat lodge ceremonies occurred in the evening."

"Our medicine man is the guide for this sweat and he prefers morning sweats," Jed explained as he led her up to her door and waited for her to unlock it. As soon as she was inside he shut her in and left.

Chapter Six

Jed sat cross-legged inside the sweat lodge, the strange toggle held loosely in his hands. Smoke from smouldering dried sage perfumed the air. There were only six participants, besides their guide, and they all chanted beneath their breath. Gradually, visions flitted across Jed's receptive mind. His spirit guide, a red-tailed hawk, first showed him where the toggle had fallen from his coat and been lost amongst the brush in Seven-mile Coulee. He'd been hunting a bear through the long narrow cut.

The next vision showed a little white boy finding the bone button when he was playing in the coulee. His mother called him and when the boy looked up Jed saw a strange flying machine in the sky. It had four straight flat wings attached to a long red body.

Still another vision blossomed and he saw the toggle being sewn onto a dark blue nurse's cape. He watched the woman fling on the cape, fasten it, then hasten out into the night. A green vehicle with a big red cross on its side awaited her. Electric lights shone down on the streets as the vehicle drove through a large town.

The final vision focused in on a little old white lady. She dumped a glass jar of buttons onto a table. Every shape and size spilled out. The yellowed toggle sat on top of the pile. She picked it up, turned it this way and that, then chuckled to herself as she pushed it into a pink crêpe paper-wrapped tube. Suddenly, she looked up and stared directly into his eyes. *"She's the one for you, Jed. Don't let her go."*

Startled, Jed jerked free of the visions, swaying so that he leaned against the Kainai elder beside him, who resolved into the medicine man, their guide for this sweat. The others had left the lodge and the space had begun to cool.

"Runs-With-the-Wind," the medicine man said, clutching Jed's arm to steady him. The inside of the lodge was almost pitch-black. "I have seen that your path is diverging. Going the way of the white man." He sighed and shifted position, removing his hand from Jed's arm. "Do not resist."

"But . . ."

"Tch, tch, tch. You will always be welcome in my lodge, Runs-With-the-Wind." He clucked his tongue and rose to his feet, bending his back to keep from hitting his head on the top of the lodge. "Bring your woman to me for a blessing. She will be made welcome."

"I..." Jed began to say, then allowed the feeling of the final vision to seep through him again. Acceptance felt right. Not easy, but right. "I will."

* * * * *

Anticipating that she would probably have visitors on Boxing Day, Sally rose early to start some baking. First she tested the oven by making dried apple and raisin oatmeal cookies. While these were baking she peeled some fresh apples and made pie crust.

While she baked, Sally pondered her situation. Here she was, magically in the past, baking cookies as if it were any other day of the week. And tomorrow night she'd have to choose a stranger to marry. She only knew two single men in this town—Doctor Robbins and Jed. The doctor had seemed nice, but he did not compare to Jed. A mountain man. Or near enough to one that it made no difference. *Imagine that.*

Sally's heart skittered just at the thought of him. She'd never before dreamed that she would be attracted to a man with a beard. Men with full beards really weren't that common in the twenty-first century, she mused, crimping the pie crust edges together. She cut a few slits into the top shell and popped the pie into the oven.

"I'll need to turn that halfway through," Sally murmured

to herself, checking her wrist. She patted the spot where her watch should be and said a soft, "Darn." She stepped across the room so that she could see the mantel over the fireplace where a wooden case clock sat. She noted the time and returned to tidying up the kitchen. She'd have to get herself a new wristwatch and then remembered how her grandmother had explained that the soldiers in World War One had tied their pocket watches onto their arms, creating the first wristwatches. *Okay, a pocket watch, then. There was probably one in the Sears catalogue.* Sally refused to make a list of conveniences that she would miss, however.

"O, that way madness lies," she said aloud—one of her favorite quotes from King Lear. "Let me shun that; No more of that."

By ten o'clock the visitors began to arrive. Most just said hello on the front porch, so Sally offered each visitor a cookie from a basket she kept beside the door. She'd made five dozen—losing only a dozen or so because of burning—and by lunch she had only a dozen left. Her pie had turned out well, though she'd almost forgotten to rotate it after half an hour. The townsfolk had all been very welcoming, but with each knock on her door her pulse had shimmied in anticipation of Jed's promised visit.

* * * * *

When Jed stopped his horses outside the teacher's house later that day he saw that smoke curled out of both chimneys. He climbed down from the sled and nodded at the two women standing on the porch. They'd obviously just left the teacher.

"Mrs. Chaplinski. Mrs. Smolak," Jed said, touching the edge of his fur hat in respect. These two matrons had been the most vocal in insisting that a teacher be brought to their growing town. They each had six children under the age of twelve. "I hope you are havin' a pleasant Boxing Day."

"Preacher," they said in unison and nodded their assent. Mrs. Smolak added, "I see you've been to the barber this morning."

"Yes, ma'am," Jed said, stroking his trimmed beard. "How is the new teacher getting on today?" he asked, stepping aside for them to join him in the street.

"We've brought her a list of the children who should be in school come Monday morning," Mrs. Chaplinski explained in her heavily accented English. She and her husband had emigrated from the Ukraine four years before. Mrs. Smolak's Polish accent wasn't much better. Both ladies fitted brightly patterned woollen scarves over their neatly arranged hair.

"She served us herb tea and apple pie." Mrs. Smolak smoothed the front of her black coat and sniffed. "The pie wasn't as good as dear Mrs. Chaplinski's, but it was acceptable."

"Most acceptable. The man she chooses will be fortunate," Mrs. Chaplinski added. "She's very pretty for a teacher. I hope she can keep my brood in order." She nodded to her friend. "And your lively bunch too."

"Yes." Mrs. Smolak looked way up at Jed, for she stood a full foot shorter than he. She raised her dark eyebrows high. "And, what business do you have with our new teacher? Her reputation must not suffer, Preacher, from receiving single men in her parlor."

Jed stiffened but merely jingled his pocket. "I've brought her the keys to the schoolhouse and to make certain she knows what time the meeting is tomorrow night."

"We've told her that," Mrs. Smolak said. She held out her hand for the keys. "We'll be happy to be certain she has the keys."

Before Jed could discover a reason to refuse her, or perhaps merely to stare her down, which he did very well by putting on a blank Kainai expression that usually disconcerted white folks, the front door opened and Miss Winters stuck her head out into the cold.

"Oh, Mr. Lavine. I thought I heard your sled. How fortunate that you've arrived. Do you know how to get the boiler working? I'd really appreciate it if you could take a look at the contraption. I've never seen anything like it." The teacher smiled, acknowledged the two older women, then waved Jed forward. "Quickly, now, please. There's no use heating the whole outdoors."

"Yes, ma'am," Jed said, touching his finger to his hat and nodding at the interested ladies, saying in an aside to them, "I think she'll be able to handle the children just fine."

Sally closed the door as soon as Jed entered the front room. She smiled warmly at him and indicated that he should follow her into the kitchen.

"You've trimmed your beard and hair. Very nice," she praised, then blushed. "How was your sweat?"

"It was interesting," Jed said, staring at her as he divested himself of his outerwear. The house smelled of apples and cinnamon. The remains of the pie sat on the counter beside an open copy of *Mrs. Beeton's Book of Household Management.* Today, Miss Winters had dressed again in the dark brown wool skirt, but instead of the fawn-colored blouse she'd worn the day before she wore a sky-blue one that matched her eyes. Her hair had been braided and pinned up, leaving her bangs free to frame her pretty face.

"Good. I've discovered the boiler, here, in a closet behind the range," she explained, moving away from him and opening the door. An upright, oblong copper boiler inhabited the small space. Several copper pipes extended through the wall and ran into the firebox of her coal-fired range. "I assume that the water from the boiler, once it is full of water, that is, runs through these pipes and then through the firebox and then back to the boiler. However, I'm just guessing. Do you know anything about it?"

"No." Jed looked at the copper boiler for a second, then moved back into the kitchen proper. "Bob Turner, who owns the mercantile, arranged to have a firm in Lethbridge come down and install it. He has one just like it and should be able to help you."

"I hope so," Sally said, following him. "I heated the water

on the stove this morning to wash. Thank goodness someone left me some Pears soap."

"Everyone with children, and even some without, pitched in to make certain you were supplied with dishes, utensils, food and so on," Jed explained.

An image of her bathing filled his mind and caused his loins to stir. In reaction, he crossed his arms, pulling the blue flannel shirt he wore tight over his broad shoulders, and watched her, keeping his expression carefully inscrutable.

"What is it, Mr. Lavine?" Sally asked, cautiously going to stand as close to him as she dared. She wondered if he would let her within his personal space. She knew she wanted to be there, close to him. He made her feel safe and excited at the same time and the sensation exhilarated her. Being in this time definitely had some compensations. Coping with the differences would be much easier if she had someone to guide her—someone about six feet tall and built like a Kainai warrior. "What do you do for a living, Mr. Lavine?"

"Preacher," he said. She raised her eyebrow at him. "Jed, if you prefer, ma'am."

"Very well, Jed, you may call me Sally. Will you answer my question?"

"Besides trapping, I work as a scout for the Northwest Mounted Police."

Without actually touching him, Sally managed to ease her way even closer to him. Jed held his ground, but she could hear his breathing speed up. His eyelids lowered so that he was watching her as if she were a tasty snack. She forged on.

"Does that mean you are often away from Crombly?"

"Yes. Sometimes for months at a time." Jed's reply sounded like a warning. Her hand came to rest on his folded arms and he twitched. "But, couldn't you find some other work? Couldn't you farm instead?" she asked softly, blushing under his continued stare but goaded on by the trembling she could feel under her palm where it rested on his forearm. Her insides felt all soft and melting. She wondered if he felt the same.

"I could. But, to what purpose?"

Sally's voice dropped to a sensual whisper. "Circumstances change."

"They do," Jed croaked out before he unfolded his arms and drew her within them. "They do, indeed," he murmured, even as he lowered his head and kissed her.

His lips moved over hers, tasting, nipping, savoring. She opened her lips under his tender onslaught and his tongue swept in to take possession of her. Sally shuddered beneath his touch and reached up between them so that her fingers threaded through his hair and pulled him even closer. They devoured one another as if neither had ever before found succour for their loneliness.

Sally's hands came down and stroked his beard as she broke off the kiss and tilted her head to one side so that he could press kisses to her neck. His touch drew out a gasp and she closed her eyes again in delight. She whimpered when he pushed her a little away.

"Sally," he whispered. "Enough. Enough." He released her and grasped her upper arms, holding her away from him.

Sally felt her face flush in humiliation and she tried to wrench herself away from him.

"Do not," he ordered softly. "Do not struggle so. I will not hurt you."

Sally stilled and her gaze flew to his face. "I didn't think you would."

His grip eased and he rubbed her arms. "We must control ourselves." He took a deep breath and gave her a crooked grin. "No matter how much pleasure we create."

"I feel so embarrassed," Sally confessed. She pressed her palms to her crimson cheeks. "Throwing myself at you . . ."

"I liked it," Jed revealed, smiling with his eyes.

How did he do that?

"If you put on your coat and toque we can go over to the schoolhouse," Jed suggested. "Would you like to see where you will teach?"

Sally nodded eagerly. Excitement overrode her embarrassment. "I'll get my things."

In moments they stood on the front porch, pulling the door shut. Jed took the key from her, locked the door and then he handed the key back to her.

Sally clutched the old-fashioned key in her gloved hand, feeling as if she still needed to pinch herself to believe that she stood in 1899—nearly at the start of a new century. She stuffed the key into the pocket of her heavy red wool coat. The coat hung down to her knees and had a flaring bottom that accommodated the width of her skirts.

They turned to the street and she noticed Mrs. Smolak and Mrs. Chaplinski down the road talking with the blacksmith. All three were watching them. Sally waved gaily, refusing to be unnerved. She'd lived in a small town most of her life. Jed had been right to stop their kisses. His consideration for her reputation was one more positive attribute to add to her list.

"Do you see?" Jed asked.

"I do and I thank you." Sally smiled shyly at him.

Jed smiled back. "This way."

While they trudged through the ankle deep snow to the schoolhouse two blocks away—in the opposite direction from the mayor's house—Sally looked around. Like the evening before, she was able to recognise some of the freshly built houses and buildings that she had known over one hundred years in the future. The sun shone brightly and the clear blue sky stretched from the gently undulating prairie all the way to the snow-capped Rocky Mountains. Chief Mountain, just over the border in Montana, stood out proudly. Sally paused at the bottom of the path leading to the dark green schoolhouse so that she could look more closely at Chief Mountain's distinctive face.

"It *does* look different," she murmured to herself.

"Another slide fell this last summer," Jed said, following her gaze. "The Kainai believe that when the mountain crumbles away, it will be the end of all human life."

Without thinking, Sally nodded and added, "I climbed it in

my sixteenth year. A group of us got permission from the Blackfeet Tribal Office. Our guide was a Piegan Elder. He said when he was young the summit was big enough and flat enough to play baseball on. Now look at it. I bet you could play football on top of it."

Sally felt Jed's eyes upon her.

"Do you know how strange your words are?" Jed continued before she could find the right words to answer him. "I do not know of any white woman who has climbed the sacred mountain. Only a few white men have done so."

"I…" Sally began, but she stopped when he spoke again.

"*Ninasticko* is the Centre of the World," Jed acknowledged reverently. "I spent my vision quest there."

Sally gulped back an exclamation of annoyance as she realized how closely she had come to revealing her secret. Instead, she asked, "Did you meet your spirit guide?"

"I did. It is a red-tailed hawk."

"I envy you," Sally confessed, brushing a stray lock of her hair back under her toque. "I wish I had a spirit guide. It must be very reassuring to know that there is something out there that will help you know the right way to direct your life."

"Sally," Jed said, taking her elbow and leading her up to the rectangular schoolhouse. "Do you not realize that a spirit guide is just another form of the Holy Spirit? He came as a dove to proclaim Jesus the Son of God. To me he comes as a red-tailed hawk. To my uncle he comes as a gray wolf. To the medicine man in my clan he comes as a gopher. During a vision quest, the warrior's fasting proves his determination and worth to obtain the guidance of the Holy Spirit." He stopped them at the bottom of the steps. A pleasing enthusiasm infused Jed's voice, which explained why he was commonly known as Preacher. "Women do not need a spirit guide."

"Well, and why not?" Sally demanded, pardonably annoyed. Ignoring the cold breeze that chafed at her cheeks, she stopped at the bottom of the schoolhouse steps and placed her fists on her waist, giving him her best stern glare. Then he disarmed her with his simple answer.

"Because the Great Father gifted women with intuition."

"Oh." Sally laughed softly and relented. "Thank you. I've never considered that angle before."

Jed led her up the three steps to the white double front doors of the schoolhouse. He took a key out of his pocket and fit it into the iron lock. The lock turned easily and he opened the door. They entered the cloakroom, an area that separated the main hall from the entrance.

As he pulled the door shut behind them, Jed gave her some final advice. "You must learn to trust your intuition, for that is the way the Holy Spirit talks to women. Why do you think women always seem to know things that men struggle with? Baby talk. How to comfort their families. Women seem to instinctively know what to do or to say. This gift is a mystery to men. Of course, some women listen to their intuition better than others, just as some men can access their spirit guides more easily than others."

"You are very wise, you know."

Chapter Seven

Her praise caused Jed to laugh, a great swell of sound that echoed in the new building.

"Sally, I wish that were true," he said, wiping a tear from the corner of his eye. "I haven't laughed so hard in a long time."

She laughed softly with him. She looked around the cloakroom, where coat hooks marched along the plaster walls beneath wood storage cubicles. Long wooden benches lined both walls beneath the hooks. Doorways at each end of the cloakroom led directly into the main teaching space, which was much larger than she had expected. Student desks sat piled against the side walls and the centre space had been filled with trestle tables and chairs, as if in readiness for a party or seminar.

A fat-bellied coal-burning stove dominated one corner. Upon its flat top sat a large copper kettle. Beside the stove a through-wall coal chute had been built. The top wooden flap could be opened on this side of the wall, accessing the hopper of coal that was filled from the building's exterior. Several large blackboards adorned the teaching wall. Six huge windows flooded the room with light. Kerosene lamps hung from ceiling hooks. A substantial teacher's desk sat squarely in front of the teaching wall. An upright piano and stool occupied the corner opposite the coal stove.

Jed followed her gaze to the piano. "Do you play?"

"Yes. My grandmother insisted," Sally explained. "I wanted to be cool and learn to play the drums, but she'd have none of that!"

"Cool?" Jed asked her. "I don't understand you."

"Sorry," she said, flushing. "It means popular. You know.

With my friends." She watched him tilt his head. She waved her hand, indicating that it didn't matter what "cool" meant. "I learned behind her back, though. A friend of mine—of Irish descent—was learning the Bodhran. He taught me as he learned. I don't think Grandma ever found out."

"What is a Bodhran?" Jed demanded, frowning.

"It's a hand-held drum about so big," she explained, moving around the room. "It can be played bare-handed or with a tipper—a two ended drumstick. I have a fourteen inch one. Uh, I used to have one, I mean," she amended, grimacing. "Darn. Never mind." She caught his look of concern and it warmed her.

The space reminded her of the one-room school where she'd taught for two years on a Hutterite Colony near Cardston. There, the independent religious community had built a room at one end of their milking barn where their children—ranging in age from six to fourteen—could learn to speak English and satisfy the Alberta government's requirement that all children be educated. The children started school speaking only their German dialect, Hutterisch, then they learned standard German and English in school. However, no Hutterite Colonies would be established until 1918 when they fled persecution in the United States to settle in Manitoba and Alberta.

Empty bookshelves filled the space beneath the blackboards. Three large wooden crates had been piled in one corner. On their sides *School Supplies* and *Alberta Railway and Coal Company* had been stamped.

"Did the Alberta Railway and Coal Company donate the supplies?" Sally asked, gesturing to the crates.

"Yes. The Society for Educating Our Children, of which the two women you met earlier are foundin' members, petitioned the company for their support. No one was really surprised when we succeeded. We are a determined bunch." Jed moved over to the blackboard. Several pieces of chalk had already been laid on the ledge. He picked up a piece and began drawing on the board.

"So you're a member?" Sally asked, somewhat surprised.

"Yes," he murmured, intent on his drawing. "Some of my people believe that we can return to the old ways. But times are changin'. Education is the future. How long can we remain in ignorance and still progress?"

"You'll get no argument from me," she said, then moved across the wide plank floor, skirting the tables and chairs, and stood waiting for him to move so that she could see his picture.

Jed moved aside. Sally silently considered the rather interesting drawing.

"Do you recognize it? I saw it in the sweat lodge vision."

"Uh…" Sally considered deeply and looked into Jed's dark-brown eyes. She could see that he expected an honest answer. She gulped, took hold of her courage and continued. "It looks like a bi-plane." He raised an eyebrow. "Well, a bi-plane is a flying machine."

"I've never heard of a flyin' machine afore. Are they only found in Europe?" he asked, stepping back so that he half sat on the desk. He folded his arms. "The one in my vision was flyin' over Seven-mile Coulee. Over near Lethbridge."

Sally leaned back against the blackboard, feeling a bit light-headed. *Should I tell him? Will he think I'm crazy? Will he tell everyone else? That could be disastrous.* She watched him waiting for her answer, apparently in no hurry but clearly anticipating the truth. Whatever he thought of her answer, she didn't believe he was a blabbermouth. *Here goes.*

"Flying machines haven't been invented yet—other than hot-air balloons, of course. The first fixed-wing one that flew successfully was built by the Wright brothers. Its maiden flight was—well, will be—on December 17th, 1903. Not long now, really. They're probably working on a prototype as we speak." Sally watched Jed silently digest this information. She rushed ahead, struggling to get her tenses correct. "Others have been working on various designs. Da Vinci speculated on the possibility of man's flight in the fifteenth century. However, the Wright brothers will manage to fly in a few years and that will be the beginning of an amazing era of flight. We'll even go to the moon and there's been talk of travelling to Mars." Sally said the last as a sort of "ah-hah" revelation.

When Jed's expression changed from calm listening to inscrutable, she shut her mouth, refusing to speak again until he said something. She knew enough traditionally raised Kainai to know that this could take a while. They liked to cogitate before speaking. Jerry Potts, a famous Canadian half-Kainai scout, horse trader and interpreter, had been known for his taciturn nature. He'd died in 1896. Sally imagined that Jed must have known him. *How odd is that?*

Finally, Jed took a deep breath and asked, "What year will we go to the moon? Will it be in my lifetime?"

"1969. We might live to see it. I'd be ninety-eight." Sally stared intently at him. He stared back, unblinking. Shrugging, she added, "I missed it the first time around as I hadn't been born yet. I'll probably miss it this time too. Humph."

Jed's question came using the slow, measured tones that revealed his native heritage. "How did you get here?" Obviously, in spite of his apparent calm, she'd shocked him mightily for normally his accent revealed little.

"I'm…I'm not really certain. I went to bed after midnight on Christmas Eve in the twenty-first century and I woke up at the tail end of the nineteenth. Go figure," she whispered. In a halting voice she explained about the cracker lady and the Christmas cracker—about how it contained more than it should have, including his bone toggle button and the key to the trunk he'd brought on Christmas morning.

"Hmm," was all Jed had a chance to say before the schoolhouse door opened and they heard voices in the cloakroom.

Hastily, Sally smudged her hand across the chalk image and moved away from Jed to greet the newcomers. They were other members of the committee coming to meet her. When she'd finished with the introductions and looked around for Jed, he'd left.

Chapter Eight

Sally met Jed on the boardwalk the next morning.

"Good morning," she said cautiously, pausing to give him a searching look before proceeding. "I thought I'd approach Mr. Turner and see if he's willing to give me a hand with the boiler."

"Mornin'," he rumbled. He fell into step beside her. "I was about to go see the two other spinsters—" He stopped speaking when a sound remarkably like a snort issued from her lips. "I beg your pardon?"

"Nothing. Go on."

"Hmm. Very well. As I was sayin', I was about to go see the two other—"

"—*the two other prospective brides*," Sally finished for him, using extreme emphasis so that he could not doubt her meaning. She glanced up at him and caught sight of a quickly suppressed grin. "Go on!" she snapped.

"A bit tetchy, aren't you?" Jed asked, grinning fully now. "Is it common for women in the future to be unmarried at twenty-nine?"

"Shh!" Sally looked around hastily but they had this portion of the boardwalk to themselves. "For Heaven's sake, Jed. Just blab it out where everyone can hear you, why don't you?"

"I don't think that would be a good idea," he protested lightly.

"Most decidedly *not.*"

"Very well."

She gestured with her hand. "So, as you were saying…?"

"I thought you might like to meet the other…brides…before tonight. I need to interview them," Jed explained. He touched his hat and nodded to the Mayor, who waved at them from across the street. "They are stayin' at the Reverend and Mrs. Lammers' home, since the boarding house is full of single men come to meet the ladies."

"Thank you for thinking of me, but I would really like to have hot water," Sally said, skipping a step to keep up with his longer stride. "I'll meet them tonight."

"I'll walk with you," Jed said, taking her elbow and directing her to turn onto the next street.

Sally swallowed convulsively to quell the rush of pleasure his simple touch brought. She sneaked a peek up at him to see him looking down at her. Watching her. Again. It was impossible to know what he thought, for his dark eyes revealed nothing. Finally he spoke, his voice low but throbbing with intensity.

"Will the *Niitsitapi* become absorbed by the white man and disappear? Will we lose our way entirely?"

Sally stopped. They were alone on this side of the street but she spoke quietly. "They will not be swallowed up. However, they will lose their way for a while." She winced when Jed closed his eyes. "But, they will rally and gradually, with education, both of the white man and of your people, things will begin to look up." Sally pressed his arm. He opened his eyes, revealing his distress. Hesitantly, she asked, "Were you forced to attend a...a residential school?"

Jed nodded curtly, his features hardening.

"I had it easier than most, though," he revealed in dull tones devoid of any emotion. "I was taken from my mother when I was five and sent to a Catholic school. My father was away up north. When I was taken he sent for my mother to be with him. They travelled together throughout the Athabasca District for six years. Then an illness took my mother. He buried her beside the Peace River and returned here to tell her family. That was when he discovered that the school I'd been sent to was run by Catholics."

"I take it he didn't like that," Sally said, her lips twisting into a rueful smile.

"*That* is an understatement. He was livid." Jed gave a wry laugh that eased his expression into something resembling humor. "I remember clearly the day he arrived at the school. I look a lot like him and I'm built very similar, so you can imagine the effect he had on the staff. My father stormed into the school demandin' my release. He wore buckskins, carried a rifle, and his dog was part wolf and so fierce that no one would approach him to force him to leave. When I was brought before him he grabbed me by the collar and started to drag me away. I didn't need to be dragged. I would have raced ahead of him if he hadn't been holdin' on to me. Before we could reach the gates, Father Peter, showin' more courage than I thought he had when he didn't hold a switch in his hand, jumped in front of us, rushin' to explain that they were raisin' his savage son to be a good Catholic."

"And your father, being Jewish, did not appreciate the priest's fervor?"

Jed let out of short bark of laughter. "My father didn't care if I had no religion or if I followed my mother's beliefs, but he could not abide me becoming a Christian." He shook his head at the memory. "My father growled out that he was *Jewish*, thank you, and that he'd have no son of his being raised as a damn Christian—particularly not a Catholic Christian! He shoved the priest aside and off we went. We disappeared into the bush, far from any government control."

"Something must have stuck, though, *Preacher*," Sally suggested, raising her eyebrows and tilting her head at him.

"Oh, yes. It was too late for me in that regard," Jed confessed, his expression softening. His eyes crinkled at the corners. "Father was none too pleased. However, he re-taught me Blackfoot and several other dialects that he had learned in his travels. He taught me bushcraft, then returned me to my mother's family when I turned twenty so that I could finish learning how to be a Kainai."

"You will be pleased to know, then, that eventually the government will apologize for the Residential School program."

Jed looked sharply at her. "When?"

Sally could not hold his gaze when she replied, "November of 2005."

Jed swore. He pulled away from her and stalked off. Tears welled in Sally's eyes. She ached for him and wished that she had kept her big mouth shut. Respect for him had led her to tell him the truth but now she regretted her revelations with all her heart. She leaned against a post and swiped the tears away, praying that Jed wouldn't hate her for her knowledge.

"The Mormon Elders promise that one day we—they call us Lamanites—will 'blossom like a rose'," Jed whispered from beside her, making her jump. Sally hadn't heard him return. "What do they mean by that?"

Sally shook her head and smiled wanly. "I don't know. I've never heard that expression before. Respect will grow, Jed. I promise you. As each understands the other better. But we will have to be very patient. One day, though, there will be Natives in government positions. They will be lawyers and doctors. Great athletes. Teachers and engineers. Actors, even."

Jed looked at her in surprise. She gave a watery laugh and nodded firmly. "Gradually, too, the aboriginal peoples of North America will remember and honor their heritage. They will relearn many of the old ways and they will see their value. Blackfoot will even be taught in school. So instead of being stripped of their language, children will be encouraged to learn it."

"I hope I live to see it," Jed murmured fervently. Sally kept her mouth firmly shut. Silently, he walked beside her until they reached a large two story brick building that housed the mercantile. He nodded brusquely and left her without a farewell. She watched him stride off down the road to make his meeting. His broad shoulders appeared stiff and proud. He nodded often to passersby. Her heart swelled until she felt choked by the feelings rippling through her.

"Jedidiah Pierre Runs-With-the-Wind Lavine, you just wait," she whispered beneath her breath.

Chapter Nine

Several members of the Society awaited her on the porch when Sally opened her front door that evening. Her hopes that Jed would be waiting to escort her died. However, she greeted the Society members cordially, giving no indication of her keen disappointment. One of the men took her offering—baked scalloped potatoes—for the buffet supper that was to be held before the choosing ceremony. They joined the throng heading for the new schoolhouse. A party atmosphere filled the air in spite of freshening *Chinook* winds whipping about them. The warm winds, if they kept up, would likely strip the ground of most of the snow before morning. Children ran back and forth through the crowd. Most of them managed to come close enough to their new teacher to get a look. She smiled at them. Some of them smiled back and some of them just rushed away to their mothers' sides.

Sally's stomach churned with anxious anticipation. She'd never felt so alive. This madness carried her along on its shoulders and didn't seem to want to put her down again. Time had interfered in her life for some impenetrable reason of its own and she wasn't certain she would choose to go back to her own time if the option were open to her. There was no one there who cared whether she lived or died. Sally thought she caught sight of Jed's tall figure standing at the top of the stairs, holding the door open for an elderly lady. He glanced her way and her heart leaped. So much of her future happiness depended on what happened here tonight.

Once inside, Sally met the two other single ladies. All three of them had been placed slightly apart from the group at a table of their own. Several matronly women joined them, bringing them food and glasses of dark burgundy chokecherry punch. The single men sat together as well. Sally was relieved to see that Jed had joined the single men, who all took every opportunity to glance their way. Sally saw that his choice of seat did not go unnoticed by the rest of the community and a stir went through the room.

At last, after the tables had been taken down and the chairs set in rows, the mayor stood up by the teacher's desk and said a few welcoming words, then waved to Jed to join him. Jed stood up and moved over to stand by the teacher's desk. The mayor returned to his wife's side. The three women under scrutiny sat behind the desk.

Jed wore a white shirt, a black string tie and black wool trousers. Over the white shirt he wore a fawn-colored leather waistcoat embroidered across the back and the shoulders with intricate quill work. His dark curls had been combed and brushed back from his handsome face. He clapped his hands a few times and waited for the room to fall silent.

"Welcome to the Choosing meetin'." Jed waved to the three ladies. "I've been charged with introducin' our three honored guests. Miss Carlyle?"

Miss Carlyle stood up and smiled cheerfully at the gathering. She was a buxom, sturdy looking woman of above average height. Her hair was a vivid shade of copper-red. Her round face had been liberally gifted with freckles and her blonde eyebrows and eyelashes appeared non-existent. When she smiled, her teeth were seen to be slightly crooked in the front but otherwise not unattractive.

"Miss Molly Carlyle is twenty-six years old and grew up on a farm in Ireland. Her family immigrated to Cape Breton Island when she was sixteen. When the railroad came through to the Alberta District, Miss Carlyle decided that this was her chance to see the Wild West." Jed paused to allow a chuckle or two to subside. Molly blushed beet red. "She knows how to work a plough, milk cows, ride a horse and accomplish all types of housewifery." A positive stir went through the room and several of the single men and a good number of the married women were nodding in approval. Molly reached over and tugged on Jed's sleeve. He turned to listen to her whisper. He nodded and then turned back to add, "Miss Carlyle can also read and write and do figures. She's Catholic."

Miss Carlyle smiled at everyone once more, then sat down. Jed nodded to the next single lady. This lady proved to be a mannish sort of woman who looked as if she'd been forced into the ill-fitting gray flannel dress she wore. Her dark hair was short and dead straight. Black eyebrows, surprisingly slender, slashed across her brow. A strong nose and jaw jutted forward belligerently. Her expression was pugnacious, as though too many disappointments had been her lot and this was going to be another one. Her stormy gray eyes glared at the single men. Some of them snickered behind their hands. Jed knocked on the desk, calling for their attention.

"This is Mrs. Anne Mackenzie. She is thirty-one years old and she was widowed when she was twenty-two. Her husband was a trapper and a guide. Her father was also a trapper and a guide for the Northwest Company near Fort St. James on the other side of the Rockies, so she's been raised with a good deal of bushcraft knowledge. She's a fine shot, which I've tested myself," Jed added. "She can speak some Salish, which I can also verify. Also, she knows some of the language of the Chipewyan peoples. Mrs. Mackenzie also comes with a riding horse and two fine, sturdy pack horses. She's not religious."

"But can she cook?" someone called out from the audience. Everyone laughed.

Anne's hands fisted at her sides and rose to rest on her hips. "I can!"

There were continued snide comments between some of the men and a few titters from some women. Jed waved at them to be silent, a heavy frown marring his brow, but they ignored him. Suddenly, a piece of chalk sailed across the room and struck a nasty man in the middle of his forehead. His yowl drew everyone's attention.

"Now," Sally said firmly, her normally soft voice carrying robustly across the space. She stood as tall as her five-feet-four allowed her to be, her back ramrod straight. "We have had quite enough of *that* sort of behavior." The outraged teacher pointed at the back of the hall. "If you have nothing decent to say for yourself, you may leave." Everyone fell silent. A few feet shuffled and chairs creaked, but no one rose. "Very well. Mr. Lavine? Please, continue."

"Thank you, Miss Winters," Jed said, his eyes flickering over her. He contained his smile, however, and turned back to Mrs. Mackenzie. "Thank you, ma'am. Please remain standin'. Miss Carlyle? Please, stand up again."

The two women came and stood one to each side of Jed.

"Miss Winters is a special case in that only single men already livin' in Crombly, or willin' to move here, may stand for her choice. If all the single men will please rise who have come for one of these two women and introduce yourselves."

"I'm J-Jeremy W-Woodruf," the first man stuttered. He had a full beard and wore a black wool suit, but was clearly a farmer of about thirty years of age. "I have a f-f-farm d-down in the new town of S-S-Stirling. I have a c-couple of pigs, three milking c-cows, and a d-d-dozen ch-chickens."

"And you're Mormon, aren't you?" Jed pointed out in a matter-of-fact voice.

"I am," came Jeremy's proud response.

"Next," Jed said.

Seven other men stepped forward and introduced themselves and stated their circumstances. One last man rose from his seat at the end of a row. He was older than the rest, at least forty years old. His hair had started to -gray and he had a large- gray handlebar moustache. He wore fringed buckskins and must have stood over six feet in his stockings. His size was impressive and his piercing blue stare passed over Miss Carlyle and settled firmly on Mrs. Mackenzie.

"My name is Jon Johanson. I don't know if you remember me, Mrs. Mackenzie, but I knew your father." Respect tinged his gravelly voice. "He was a good man." She nodded her thanks and waited for him to continue. He looked away from her and swept the crowd with his penetrating gaze before returning it to Mrs. Mackenzie. "No offence to all of you, but the District of Alberta is getting far too crowded for me. I'm looking to move north into the District of Athabasca. Perhaps into the Peace River region. Or maybe we'll settle over near Fort Chipewyan on Lake Athabasca. I'd be pleased if you'd be willing to come with me as my wife."

"I accept your offer," was her simple reply. He nodded brusquely and sat back down. Mrs. Mackenzie returned to her own seat, clearly proud to have the matter settled so quickly.

Sally leaned close to her and whispered, "*Do* you remember him?" Anne nodded. "And do you like him?"

"He's an excellent shot," Anne whispered back.

"Oh," Sally murmured, trying not to be shocked. Different times, different thinking.

"He's always been respectful of others," Anne added, seeming to feel that Sally needed more reassuring.

"That's an excellent quality," the teacher praised. "Felicitations." Anne nodded smugly.

"Miss Carlyle, do you have a preference?" Jed asked, waving at the eight men still standing.

"I liked the first one, so," Molly Carlyle said boldly, though she blushed furiously and looked shy. "His stammerin' doesn't bother me none because m'brother was jist such a stammerin' one as this. I pray my accent will prove pleasin' to him."

"Now, ma'am, I hope you understand that Jeremy's a Mormon and Stirling is a Mormon town so there'll not be a priest there for you," Jed cautioned. "On the plus side, he doesn't drink or chew tobacco or smoke."

Jeremy had been grinning from ear to ear but he sobered and waited to hear her answer, which took long enough to come for him to start worrying.

"I'll convert," she stated finally, then hastily crossed herself and muttered, "May God forgive me." A ragged laugh sounded from the gathered townsfolk. "And m'family too," she added, gulping. Molly grasped Jed's sleeve. "What do you think, Preacher? Will it be all right, so?"

Jed covered her hand with his and smiled down into her

homely but kindly countenance. "Jeremy Woodruff is as gentle a man as you could hope to meet, Miss Carlyle. He's hard working, loves the Lord and treats his friends well. I think he's even got all his teeth."

"I d-do," Jeremy managed to get out, grinning widely and showing a fine set of teeth, though one front upper tooth had a chip out of it.

"So, and I'll be pleased to be wed to him," Molly said, then laughed a bit and said, "For I've got all m'teeth too!"

Everyone laughed and the tension eased. Miss Carlyle returned to her seat, smiling widely and sneaking shy looks at her husband-to-be.

Chapter Ten

"Miss Winters. Will you stand, please?" Jed asked, nodding so impassively at her that Sally wondered if she'd frightened him off with her earlier revelations. Taking her courage by the throat, Sally rose and moved to stand at his side. She clasped her sweating hands in front of her and submitted to the scrutiny of the group.

"Our new teacher is twenty-nine years old. The man she chooses will have a fine new house to live in, containing many modern conveniences," Jed stated.

Sally's insides twisted as she watched the lecherous and greedy looks being exchanged between some of the men. She glanced up at Jed, wondering if he'd noticed or even cared. His jaw looked clenched. Promising.

"These include running water, both hot and cold."

"Once Mr. Turner and I get the boiler working, that is," Sally chimed in. She tried to control her embarrassment for she felt as if she were being put up for auction. Going once, going twice... Fortunately she already knew her choice.

"*I'm* doing the introductions," Jed whispered.

"Then get a move on," Sally hissed back. "Say something nice about me, not about my bloody house!"

Through gritted teeth, Jed continued, "She's a quick learner. When she first arrived she didn't know how to start a coal fire. Now she does."

People laughed and Sally wanted to kick him. Before Jed could speak again—damning her with faint praise—she addressed the room herself.

"Though I've never milked a cow or looked after chickens—" More astonished gasps greeted that information. She ignored them. "I have kept sheep and I have sheared them.

I know how to prepare the fleece, spin, weave, knit and crochet." Sally cast a self-satisfied look at Jed when the townsfolk nodded their approval. "I can speak German, French, and—" Jed took her elbow and squeezed it. "And some Dutch," she amended, wondering why he didn't want her to reveal that she spoke some Blackfoot. Probably because she had no way to explain her knowledge. "I am also confident in my homemaking skills. If you liked the scalloped potatoes tonight, that was *my* dish."

"And she's mighty perty too!"

Jed stepped forward ominously, but before he could speak, Mrs. Smolak jumped up and rounded on the disreputable-looking man.

"Will Switchin!" she barked. "You mind your manners." She folded her arms over her ample bosom and glared. "I don't know why you two came over from Fort Kipp. We don't want the likes of you living in Crombly!"

"It's an open choice, ma'am," Will retorted. He rose and pushed his way forward, his friend following behind. Neither looked as if he'd bathed in months. "We've as much a right to be here as any of the others." He cast an indignant look over Jed. "And more rights than some."

"Yah," his friend said, right before he prepared to spit a wad of tobacco on the floor.

"You'd better not," Sally warned menacingly.

She startled the man so much that he swallowed his foul spit, causing him to cough mightily. The other single men pulled the troublesome two down onto chairs and kept firm hands on their shoulders. Jed indicated to those he knew were interested to stand and introduce themselves. Sally calmly listened to what they had to offer her. Doctor Robbins had included himself in the group. Most of them seemed respectable individuals. However, she didn't want any of them. This choosing could have only one result as far as she was concerned.

"Thank you all for introducing yourselves and offering to be my husband," Sally said, nodding to each of them. "I am honored. However, before I make my choice, I'd like to say thank you to everyone who has given me food and goods so that my new home was ready for me. I truly appreciate it."

Jed watched smiles wreath the community members' faces. His knees felt weak and his heart was racing, for Sally had not given any indication that she considered him a candidate for her hand. He knew that no one would expect it as he'd made his position clear when he'd told everyone he wasn't looking for a wife. The red-tailed hawk's screech echoed across his soul. He turned to look at Sally and discovered that she was looking at him. Her blue eyes appeared huge and he felt as if he were drowning in them.

"So, now that the time to make my choice has come," she was saying… He held his breath. "I'm going to go by my intuition." Jed's eyes narrowed as he remembered their conversation on the schoolhouse steps. "And so, I choose—" Jed could hear the roaring of his blood through his veins. Her intuition! All other sounds faded away. "—Jedidiah Lavine to be my husband." The room again erupted with sound.

"But he's a damn injun!" Will Hitchin exclaimed. He jabbed a dirty finger at Jed. "He might look white, teacher, but he ain't."

"So I understand," Sally replied. She felt his hand searching for hers and they twined their fingers together. His stony expression was back and she could feel the tension in him. "His racial heritage does not deter me."

"I'm Ben Moss, ma'am." A stubby gray-haired man rose to his feet at the urging of his equally short and rotund wife. "I own the livery stables. I'm sorry to have to tell you this, Miss Winters." He spoke hesitantly. "Even though he talks of Jesus in his sermons…Preacher, here, is a Jew." He held up a placating hand. "Now, Preacher, I don't got nothin' against you, you know that, but truth is truth."

The congregation all nodded. Sally shook her head at them. They insisted on nodding at her again. She pursed her lips and waited for Jed to defend himself. Instead he just stood there, stiff and silent.

"I beg to differ with you, Mr. Moss," explained Sally patiently. "Unless Jed's mother converted to Judaism before he was born, or Jed converted himself, then he is not a Jew, even though his father was one."

"Eh?" was the general feeling in the room.

"She's right," Mrs. Chaplinski insisted. "*Tak*, she is. In my old village back in Ukraine, there lived Jewish families. I tell you, she is right."

"Regardless," Sally said loudly over the din. "Regardless. I have no objection to Mr. Lavine's religious heritage, either. My understanding of the contract is that the town promises me a husband and I have to choose one. I've chosen. Mr. Lavine and I will suit each other just fine. If he is agreeable, then let us proceed with the weddings."

"I am agreeable," came Jed's quiet but firm reply.

"Yes. Let's get on with it!" Anne Mackenzie said, rising to her feet.

Anne came and stood beside Jed and Jon Johanson joined her. She looked surprised and gratified when he threw his arm around her and hugged her to his side.

"So, and I'm agreeable too," Molly Carlyle said, and moved over beside Sally. She held out her hand to Jeremy and he scooted across the floor to stand beside her. He grinned up at her, for she topped him by an inch or so and outweighed him by a few pounds. She tucked her hand through his arm and drew him to her. He patted her hand and faced the room.

The Reverend Lammers did the honors. He asked every couple in turn whether they would accept each other as their spouses. Molly, grinning as wide as could be, stated clearly for all to hear that she'd be delighted. Jeremy laughed softly as though equally delighted to be her husband and then declared in a solemn voice that he'd be right privileged.

Anne's response seemed wooden and she actually looked the most frightened of the three even though she'd been married before. Jon held her trembling hand between both of his large ones. In a strong, thoughtful voice he swore to be a good husband and to honor his new wife.

Sally's answers to the Reverend's questions sounded breathless to her but she filled them with anticipation. Jed's replies were spoken in a voice so deep and calm that she doubted if half of the room could hear him. Sally heard him, though, as did the Reverend, and that is what counted most.

Dancing followed, the music being supplied by a fiddler and an accordion player. Everyone wanted to dance with the brides and it was several hours before the couples were able to pull away from the celebration, each to their own marriage bed.

Chapter Eleven

The pretty new house seemed warm and cosy to Sally as they stepped through the front door and into their home. They closed the door behind them, locked it, then stood in the very dim glow of the coals in the fireplace.

"I thought I'd scared you off," Sally murmured, feeling nervous and odd. She went over to the fireplace and added some fuel to it. She heard a match strike and flare, and when she turned she could see Jed lighting the glass lamp on the cherrywood table.

"What is this?" he asked, pointing at the torn open pink Christmas cracker.

"It's the cracker I told you about."

"It's broken. Why do you still have it?" Jed's dark eyes pierced hers. "Do you hope that it will return you to your own time?"

"I...maybe I did," Sally admitted. She gathered up the bits. "But not anymore. When I chose you, I chose this time too." And she tossed the crêpe paper-wrapped tube into the fire.

Sally remained standing with her back to Jed, looking at the flames. She started when she felt his hands come around her and pull off her heavy coat. She heard him move away and when he returned to draw her backward into his arms she could tell that he'd removed his outerwear too. He rested his chin on her shoulder and they stared at the flames together.

"You look very beautiful tonight," he whispered against the soft skin of her neck. She shivered. Jed stepped back and began to remove her hairpins. He gently arranged her long hair about her shoulders.

"Your hair is the color of ripe grain."

Sally turned around so that she could touch him. He held still while her fingers fumbled with his buttons. As soon as she had them open, she pulled on one end of his string tie, releasing the bow. An anticipatory smile hovered on her lips and she held her breath when she pushed his shirt off his chest. The gray vest of his long johns was the only thing revealed. Her pout of disappointed elicited a chuckle from Jed. Sally blushed, then attacked the additional buttons.

"I want to see you," Sally begged.

He grinned and pushed her hands aside.

"Here, let me," Jed murmured.

In a trice he had his vest, shirt and tie off. He kicked off his boots. He stared into her eyes as he stripped off the remainder of his clothes. His dark gaze burned with eager desire and Sally's own embers flared even higher. After taking off his socks, he stood there boldly before her and she admired his well-muscled body.

"Do you like what you see?"

"Oh, yes," Sally whispered.

Her hands reached out to trace the shape of his chest. The palm of her hand slid across his nipples and she sighed when he started in surprised pleasure. When her searching touch encountered the full, hard velvety length of him, he groaned.

"We've got to get your clothes off too," he rasped, and his voice sounded hungry.

They fumbled and laughed together while they removed layer after layer of her feminine garb. Jed uttered a soft curse or two. Sally suspected that he'd never made love to a white woman before and had had no idea of the innumerable obstructions between his hands and her bare skin.

At last his wife stood revealed to his appreciative gaze. Her breasts were small but perfectly formed with large dark tips that stood out against her creamy white skin. Her narrow waist curved down to slender hips. His hands trembled as he gently traced the soft skin of her hips around to her full, rounded bottom. He laughed softly and lifted her up so that they touched warm skin to warm skin. He nestled his erect member between her soft thighs while his mouth took possession of her full lips.

His lips were gently persuasive as they moved over hers and when his tongue traced the outline of her lips she opened eagerly to his inquiry. Jed tasted of her sweetness and was lost. Diving into her warm invitation, his tongue stroked hers, then her teeth, then the top of her mouth, coaxing a tiny whimper of response from her. Sally opened to him by raising her legs so that they wrapped around his hips.

"Huh," he gasped, tearing his mouth from hers as he felt her hot, moist invitation against him. He adjusted her hips and then surged into her waiting fire. She gave a startled exclamation and he stilled. She felt tight—much tighter than he'd expected.

Sally fell through a vortex of feelings and sensations and she latched onto his tongue and sucked it into her mouth, stroking it with her tongue. She could feel his pulsing length between her thighs and she squeezed him tight while she clutched his wide shoulders. There was no way to describe adequately the emotions that surged through her as she celebrated in the achingly amazing sensation of naked skin pressed to naked skin. Heat gushed forth from her womanly centre, easing their union.

"I'm okay," she promised, savoring the fullness within her. "Oh, yes. It's just been a long time, that's all." She experimentally tilted her hips forward, taking even more of him inside her. She let out a long, shuddering breath. "Please, don't stop."

"I don't think I could stop," he panted.

He kept firm hold of her hips and lowered her to the rug. Resting his elbows on either side of her, he gently stroked her hair out of her face and kissed her with exquisite tenderness. Tears formed as she watched him through half-closed lids.

Revelling in the hot, silky feel of his skin, she smoothed her hands across his shoulders and then down between them.

She mischievously tweaked his sensitive nipples between her thumbs and forefinger.

Gradually increasing his pace, Jed thrust his member into her again and again. She matched his escalating fervor by rising to meet each plunge. Her breasts swayed back and forth across his hard chest, rubbing her own sensitive nipples. She felt mad with sexual craving and gulped in great heaving breaths.

The world spiralled out of control as Sally felt her release come upon her. She screamed softly and tightened around him.

Jed's release came as hers ebbed so she felt every pulse of his pleasure. This new and powerful sensation seemed to go on and on as he shuddered above her. They collapsed together and he turned them to their sides so that he could nestle her against his chest as they gasped and shook occasionally while they recovered.

Tears tumbled off of Sally's eyelashes as she whispered, "That was the most amazing thing. Ever." Some of her emotion must have shown in her voice for Jed rolled her over a bit so that he could see her eyes. She bit her lip and blushed under his scrutiny. He brushed her tears away and kissed both her eyes. Sally threw her arms around his neck and hugged him fiercely. "I love you, Jedidiah Pierre Runs-With-the-Wind Lavine."

"Is it possible? For you to love me in such a short time?" Jed asked, holding his breath as he hugged her back. "Are you sure? It's not just the after-effects of our passion?"

"I am sure. So very, very sure," she whispered ardently. "Our passion is a result of our feelings, not the cause of them."

"I'm very glad of it," Jed confessed, stroking the soft skin of her back. "Because I also love you."

Sally drew back and beamed at him. The beauty of the love shining out of her eyes made his heart ache. Again he heard the screech of the red-tailed hawk. Once more his spirit guide had led him to a good place. Home.

"You know, when I first met you I thought you were a

throw-back to the mountain men of the nineteenth century." She laughed and shook her head. "How little did I know then."

"When I first met you," Jed revealed, considerate and solemn. "I thought that you were very pretty. For a white woman."

"For a white woman?" Sally scoffed, chuckling. "And now?"

"Ah," Jed sighed, giving her a crooked grin. "I think you are more beautiful than the most beautiful Kainai maiden I have ever seen."

"Thank you. High praise, indeed," she murmured, then leaned forward for a kiss. His lips had her panting again in no time.

Jed lifted his wife into his arms and rose to his feet. He pressed her close to his heart as he carried her through the open bedroom door into the cooler space beyond. He flicked back the covers and set her reverently down onto the cold sheets. Sally gasped and quickly pulled his warm self down into her arms, then wrapped her legs around him. Jed covered them both with her quilts. They lay quietly enjoying each other's closeness for a long while before Jed spoke.

"Did you meet Brad Cornforth tonight?"

Sally frowned in thought and then shook her head.

"He's a representative of the Alberta Railway and Coal Company," Jed explained. He brushed her hair out of her face and kissed her forehead. "He's offered me a job working for them. It seems their man south of Lethbridge is being transferred and they need someone to replace him. I'd be travellin' around lots, still, but I wouldn't be away for months at a time like now."

"Do you think this work will suit you?" Sally asked, rubbing her cheek against his bare shoulder. He shrugged, a movement which she rode out without lifting her head.

"I won't know until I try it."

Sally lifted herself up so that she leaned her folded arms on Jed's chest and she could look down into his face. The glow from the lamp in the front room sparked in her blue eyes.

"This job will move you farther from your people into the white man's world," she noted softly. "Is that what you want?"

"Our medicine man said that my path was moving away from the Kainai and into the world of the white man. He wants me to accept the change," Jed revealed. The shadow of the hawk crossed his soul and he felt at peace.

"How long is my contract with the town?"

"Five years."

"Then, this is what I propose," she said, "If you take this job for five years, and find that you do not like it, or wish to move on, then we could perhaps move up north and homestead near Red Deer. As I recall, there are large Métis communities in that region, aren't there?"

"There are." Jed took her face between his large hands and held her still while he searched her expression. "That would be another big move for you. From twenty-first century to nineteenth and then from Crombly where you have a comfortable home, to homesteadin' where the comforts will be few."

"Fear not. I'm tougher than I look," Sally promised, smiling lovingly at him. "I will be happy wherever you are. I love you that much, you see."

Jed crushed her to him. His feelings threatened to overcome him but he managed to croak out, "As I love you."

Epilogue

The realtor waited on the front porch for the couple who strolled up the walk. They paused about halfway up to stare searchingly at the old farmhouse.

"Good afternoon," she called out. The handsome, obviously affluent young people smiled at her and came forward. "I hope you like the house."

"My sister and I aren't really here to buy. We've come down to look at the house because our great-great-grandparents used to live here."

"Really?" the realtor said, willing to chat with them since the open house had been slow. Fewer and fewer people wanted to live in the smaller Southern Alberta towns.

"Yes. Our grandmother was the first school teacher in Crombly," the young woman said. Her blue eyes looked startling with such dark hair. "Her journals have spoken about this house. It's where she was living when she married our great-great-grandfather."

"Well, come on in and look around. The house has been restored by the current owner's parents, so it looks a lot like it probably looked when it was first built," the realtor said, leading them through the front door. "There are one and a half baths, now, of course. Though you do have to go through the enclosed back porch to get to the full bath."

"Yes, we know," the older brother said. His curly blond hair made him seem almost angelic. They were both very attractive, healthy-looking siblings.

The realtor puzzled silently over that response but let it go. She followed them as they moved through the house, whispering to themselves. "Look at this," one would say. "Just like she wrote," the other would say.

"When we were preparing this house to be sold," the realtor said, pointing to a pink poke bonnet sitting on the end of the iron bedknob of the master bedroom, "we found this bonnet."

They smiled at the lost bonnet, which their great-great-grandmother had cursed over in her journals, since it was the last magical piece of the Christmas cracker. On the morning after their wedding, Sally had found that the tissue paper bonnet had transformed into a real cotton poke bonnet, which she'd worn for years before it had been lost.

"Our grandma's journal spoke of how much her grandmother missed the bonnet when they moved up to Red Deer to homestead," the young woman said, reverently picking up the bonnet. "She finished up her five-year contract with the town, you see, and they moved to Red Deer, where there was a growing Métis community. My great-great-grandfather was half-Kainai."

"This information is amazing," the realtor said. "I'm so thankful you came today. I love to have background information on the houses I sell."

"Who owns it now?" the brother asked with studied casualness.

"It's a sad story, really. The owner, also a teacher, coincidentally, disappeared over the Christmas holidays last year. She didn't show up for school when it started again. No one knows how long she'd been gone. She's not been found yet. The town has seized the house, citing an old leasing arrangement dating back to the late nineteenth century. The money earned by the sale will be put back into the school district."

"Strange," the sister said, turning away to give her brother a secret smile. "Very strange. She was a clever woman, our grandmother. It is interesting to see the humble beginnings of the dynasty she began. How much does the town want for the house?"

When the realtor told them the figure, they pursed their

lips and went into a huddle.

"Does it come with the contents?" the brother asked. The realtor nodded. They went back into a huddle. A minute later they turned back to her, smiles wreathing their faces.

"We'll take it."

The End

Jessica L. Jackson

A Viking Christmas

Author's note: Silje is pronounced like Seelya

Prologue

Aunty scooped her red and black brindle guinea pig off the corner of her worktable and set him on the crook of her arm. She stroked his long hair and shuffled over to the diamond-paned windows. Lacy frost tracings almost obscured the view of her snow-covered back garden. Jeffry purred.

"You're not a cat, you know," Aunty muttered. Her brow furrowed and her thin lips lifted at one side. "It's time, Jeffry. Time for another special Christmas cracker."

Jeffry responded with a chortle.

"No, not a woman this time. A man. Yes. The cracker will be for a man," Aunty replied.

She whipped around and returned to her worktable. Jeffry landed on his spot and whistled.

"Excited, are you?" Aunty asked, carefully gathering up the brightly adorned, but ordinary, crêpe-paper crackers and placing them in a box to one side. "Me too."

Aunty's gnarled fingers hovered over the terra cotta pots lined up on the table. Each one held an assortment of decorations for the cracker.

"Gold poinsettias, I think," she whispered, dipping her hand into one pot and emerging with three tiny silk flowers.

From another collection she gathered a golden bead chain.

She snipped off a short length and put it with the flowers. A pile of artificial greenery provided the setting for the flowers. She ran her fingers through curly ribbon strands cascading from spools attached to the dark beams overhead. "Gold, I think. Hmm, everything is gold. I hadn't expected that."

Jeffry chirped.

"What?" Aunty cocked her head to one side and observed her companion. "Yes, I've already decided to choose a dark color for the cracker body."

Jeffry switched to wheeking.

"Black?" She turned and faced the dowels holding crêpe paper in many colors. Aunty scratched a spot on her ample waist and considered her options. "Hmm. I think you're right there, Jeffry." She took a sheet of black paper and set it on her worktop. "If it's going to be black, then I'm going to have to choose..." Her hand riffled through a pile of pre-cut decorative sheets of shiny paper. "Yes, this one," she whispered, and chanted beneath her breath as she smoothed it out.

Aunty lifted one hip and rolled her hips back and forth until she'd levered her bulk up onto the wooden stool behind her table. She leaned on the surface, lifting her hips, and then settled comfortably back down. During this operation, Jeffry bubbled and purred encouragement.

With each cut, wrap, and glue, she hummed and whispered and sometimes shouted enchantments that went with each element of the Christmas cracker. When the moment came to fill the tube with prizes, she swiveled in her perch and examined the pile she'd collected earlier.

"Yes, he's going to need this for certain," she murmured, picking up the first item. She set it to one side. "And this too. And he better have this one."

Jeffry chirped.

"No, he doesn't need a sword. He already has one." She peered at him over the top of her half-moon glasses. "Besides, how do you expect me to get a sword inside a four-inch tube? Heavens, that would be a trick and a half." Aunty clicked her tongue and went back to collecting, placing an eight-inch bone flute on top of the pile. She shook a finger at the guinea pig. "Now, no noise out of you, Mister Jeffry sir. I've got to concentrate or else I'm never going to get all this inside the cracker."

Jeffry released a single chirp and then kept his mouth shut when the room darkened and the chanting began again. This time, Aunty sang her charms so that her intonations rose and fell melodically. She finished her spell with a resounding clap of her palms. She sat still, breathing deeply for many long moments. Jeffry chirped again.

"I'm fine. Don't you be worrying about me. Okay. It's time to close this beauty."

Aunty tied the second ruffle around one end, sealing off the black and gold Christmas cracker. She checked that the snap ends remained in place and then she set it before her, admiring her handiwork.

"This will do nicely," she said, smiling. "What do you think, Jeffry?"

The guinea pig commenced to wheeking, adding hopping up and down and twirling in a circle.

Aunty laughed and laughed and when she detected a cackle she stopped and covered her mouth with the back of one hand.

"Oops," she said, grinning.

Chapter One

Be silent! They have hearing like wolves!

Silje clamped a cold hand over her mouth, forcing the breath through her nose. She pressed her back against the broad trunk, willing the *Skræling* warriors to go in another direction. Her chest heaved and her knees trembled.

How much longer can I evade them?

Her hand clenched and unclenched around the handle of her seax where she held it against her chest, point down. Besides her bow and arrows, left behind where she'd been gathering fallen nuts, the long blade was the only weapon her father, the chieftain of their clan, would let her carry. In spite of her diligent practice with a sword too heavy for her, he continued to refuse to have the blacksmith make her a sword suited to her height and strength. Such rage filled her now at his injustice. When she needed to defend herself against these *Skræling* warriors who objected to the Norse band on their lands, Silje had nothing but her wits and a knife two hand-spans long to keep her alive.

A twig snapped near-by. Silje stilled, resisting the urge to close her eyes. Resisting the urge to look around the tree and see. Resisting the urge to run.

Why was I such a fool? Why did I separate myself from the others?

Silje waited until her breathing returned to normal and her knees stopped their trembling. She listened. The winter forest lay dormant and hushed. The unusually warm weather had melted the snow, leaving the forest floor litter flat and damp—slippery under fleet foot.

Thunk.

The trunk vibrated behind her.

A high, ululating cry sliced the air.

And Silje ran.

* * *

Liam bounded down the long back steps leading from the apartment he rented on the top floor of the century-old house. This was home-base. Campbellton, on the northern provincial border between New Brunswick and Quebec, was central to the region where he hoped to find evidence of a Norse presence over one thousand years in the past. This was the area, he was sure of it. His Archaeological doctoral thesis depended on his thorough examination of the clues, or the lack thereof.

It's here. I know it. I feel it in my bones.

Feeling things in his bones was a family trait handed down from grandfather to son and then to Liam. An Irish thing. Both his father and grandfather had passed on to the next life, but this legacy remained. The feeling could not be explained away with science or common sense. Liam had learned to embrace it at his grandfather's knee.

Today felt special too. He and his friend were attending a re-enactment fair being held in the barns and paddocks of a local farm. The unseasonably warm December weather was an unlooked for bonus. The snow from earlier in the month was almost gone. In a few days it would be Christmas and it looked to be a "brown" one this year.

Charlie's blue rusty pick-up idled on the street and Liam could see his hand tapping against the steering wheel. Re-enactment fairs were not Charlie's idea of a great way to spend a Saturday—which was surprising actually, considering he was an amateur actor. He'd only agreed to come because they'd known each other since elementary school. Friendships that long acquired obligations.

Liam opened the door and slid onto the duct-tape repaired seat. "Morning."

"It is."

Liam fastened his seatbelt and glanced at Charlie. His shock of shaggy dark-red hair hung over his well-freckled pale skin. A scraggly full beard attested to his determination to go unshaven until the end of hockey season.

"You look like the man of the mountains," Liam observed, grinning. They were both big men but it looked like Charlie had bulked up. "Aren't you going to cut your hair either?"

"Nope."

"You got the taciturn bit down pat. You're going to get that part for certain. It's a good thing it calls for a beard or you'd be screwed."

Bright blue eyes turned to Liam. A twinkle accompanied his grunt. "Yep. Been workin' on it."

"You're just a Canadian redneck."

"Been watchin' Mountain Men on the telly."

"If only you chewed tobacco. You could spit before you spoke."

"Dirty habit, that."

Liam chuckled. "You're going to fit right in at the fair. We should get you outfitted with a Norseman's costume."

Charlie glanced at him again before pulling out into traffic. He snorted. "Seems like that's the pot callin' the kettle black."

Liam stroked his beard. It was tight to his face and well-trimmed—not too much more than a decent five-o'clock shadow. He always let it grow in when he planned a camping trip. Shaving in the woods was too much of a headache.

"I start out tomorrow. I'm determined to take advantage of this weather so I can examine those places my bones tell me will yield the greatest rewards."

"Yer bones, eh?"

"Yer? Really?"

"Too much?"

"I don't know. Maybe."

"Yer feels right."

"Then you've got to go with it."

"Campin' by yerself?" Charlie appeared to be sucking on the inside of his cheek so Liam waited for him to spill his next thought, chewed down to the fewest possible words. It proved to be only one. "Stupid."

"You couldn't have gone with 'unwise'? Or 'foolish'?"

Charlie's lips twitched. "Nope."

Liam snorted. "Do you know where we're going?"

His friend nodded, then asked, "Got enough gear?"

"I'm going to fully immerse myself in the Norse culture this time. I want to get into their heads, so to speak. You should understand that." Liam listened for Charlie to answer but Charlie just glanced at him. "I'm going to wear Viking clothes, use a fur sleeping bag like they used to do, carry my gear in a woven birch *neverkont,* use a flint to start my fires, and so on."

"Got all that stuff?"

"Not everything. That's what I'm hoping to find at the fair. There will be stalls selling clothes and reproduction implements."

* * *

"This is the last stall. I'm pinning all my hopes on it." Liam trudged across the paddock to a horse enclosure with a wide open front, doing double duty today as a fair stall. "I suppose I should've realized that most of the wares offered would be from Colonial times and the Middle Ages."

"Yep. Shoulda."

"You're loving this, aren't you?"

Charlie chuckled and pounded once on his back.

Liam spied a pennant showing the Norwegian colors of red, blue and white hanging from a nail to one side of the stall. "Hah, look at that! I'm in luck."

"Might be. I'm wonderin' though."

They approached the stall. An old woman minded her wares, her brilliant white hair bound beneath a starched Hardanger *skaut* headcloth. Embroidered holes and crosses decorated the band holding the white linen cloth to the woman's head. A quilted black coat, trimmed with bands of woven thread in reds, greens and off-white covered her dark-navy dress. Beneath her ample bosom, a wide woven belt cinched in the whole.

"There you are," she said cryptically, smiling at him. Her black eyes twinkled over the top of half-moon glasses. "I'd almost given up on you."

Liam smiled back. "Expecting me, were you?" He looked away from her searching gaze and examined her wares. Tunics of mustard-yellow, moss-green, and midnight-blue stacked next to long trousers of brown wool. Soft leather jerkins hung in a row from nails in the side of the stall. Hard leather belts, wool cloaks, brooches, gloves, rolled putties, and leather ankle boots added to the whole. He picked up one of the boots and held it against his foot.

"This should fit," Liam said. He looked at Charlie. "What do you think?"

"Cold."

The old woman plopped several pairs of thick socks on the table.

"There you go," Liam said, nodding at the socks. "I'll need putties too."

Two rolls of dun-colored, three-inch-wide woven wool cloth strips joined the socks.

"Fer what?" Charlie asked, lifting up a roll to examine it more closely.

"I'll wind them about my legs from the ankle up to the knee, binding the bottom of my trousers to my legs. You must have seen them before. In WWI movies?"

"Yep. I remember now."

"They'll keep the cold out."

Charlie raised his eyebrows but only said, "Sleeping bag?"

Liam glanced at the old woman but she was already leaning over and rummaging beneath the table. She dragged out a large bundle of dark-brown fur, tied closed with rawhide bindings. She placed the roll on the table beside the socks, putties and boots, holding it in place with a gnarled, liver-spotted hand.

"Bear fur. Very warm," she said, glaring at Charlie before he could make a comment.

He ducked his head, hiding his smile behind his beard-stroking hand.

"I'll also need some—"

Before he could speak his needs, the stall owner began to pile tunics, trousers, a pair of sandals, a leather jerkin, and a thick square-shaped fur-lined cloak next to the other items.

"Costly," Charlie muttered, earning him another glower.

Without looking away from him, the old woman added a hard-leather helm reinforced with wood bands. A leather chin strap kept the helm on during a fight. She added a woolen cap trimmed in fur and a long, tooled leather belt. Two sword frogs hung from the belt. One would hold a scabbard and the other would hold either another sword or an axe.

Charlie whistled at the size of the pile. He spoke his longest sentence of the day. His words contained a distinct sarcastic edge. "All you need is a sword and an axe and you'll be set."

"I already have those. And a knife. I made them myself," Liam said simply, reminding his friend that he was an amateur bladesmith. "I'm bringing my axe—it's good for all sorts—but why would I need to bring my sword?"

"Bring your sword," the old woman ordered, narrowing her gaze at Liam this time.

Liam met her eyes and his bones twitched. "Okaaay," he said, drawing the word out. "I'll bring it."

Charlie shook his head. Liam ignored him. When the bones spoke he listened.

Except for the sleeping bag, all the purchases fit inside the cloak. Liam bound it shut using the long belt, cinching it closed with the hand-forged iron buckle. Liam paid for his purchases and was about to leave when the old woman detained him.

"Merry Christmas," she said, placing a dyed-blue leather tube on the table. It was approximately eight inches long and three inches in diameter. A flap of leather closed what proved to be a tubular box. "My gift to you."

"There's no need, Aunty," Liam said, then frowned at his unexpected choice of address. *Why did I call her Aunty? That's odd.*

She grinned, squidging up her face so much that her black

eyes almost disappeared beneath wrinkles. For just a moment she looked like a Norwegian apple-doll kitchen-witch. She pressed the tube into his hand.

"I like you, Liam O'Brien," she whispered, drawing him close with the crook of her finger.

She knows my name.

Then she kissed him.

Just a swift peck on the lips.

Electricity pricked his flesh and he started back, touching his hand to his mouth.

"I've given you the gift of tongues, Liam. It will prove useful."

Her chuckle sounded too much like a cackle to him and so he merely nodded, grabbed at his purchases and nudged Charlie. They left swiftly, Charlie carrying the fur sleeping bag and Liam carrying the other bundle under his left arm while his right hand clutched the tubular box. When they reached the paddock gate, Liam hesitated and glanced back. The livestock shelter remained, but there was no sign of the old woman or her wares.

What the hell?

"You comin'?" Charlie asked, holding the gate and looking toward the row of food stalls. "Hungry."

"Uh, yes. I'm coming. Did you see...? Never mind."

They found a stall that served lamb stew and bannock. They placed their order and sat at a slab of wood being used as a makeshift table. A serving wench brought them two tankards of ale and their meal. Half-way through the stew, Charlie slowed his eating and looked at Liam.

"Gift of tongues?"

Liam set down his spoon and dug inside his coat for his phone. "That's what she said."

"Strange woman."

"You said it." Liam didn't bother telling him about her disappearing act. What was the use? He tapped a question into the phone. "Okay, here it is. Let's see—the gift of tongues is one of the gifts of the Holy Ghost that allows a person to understand languages he has not previously learned. Then there's a whole lot of business about religious use, and so forth."

"*It sounds like bunk, to me,*" Charlie said.

Liam glanced up and caught his intense stare. "*I don't know. There's been lots of evidence of it. Now that I've read these explanations, I remember seeing documentaries about the phenomenon. It seems that the most common demonstration of the gift is the interpretation of religious fervor-type blathering.*"

"When did you learn German?"

"German?" Liam asked, frowning. "What are you talking about? You know I only took French in school. You're the one who took French *and* German."

"And you've never learned it since?"

"No."

"Are you putting me on?"

"Charlie," Liam said sharply. "What's this about? I don't speak German."

"*You do now.*"

"*No I don't.*" Liam heard his response this time and shut his mouth with a snap. Then, in a whisper, he added, "*Ach mein Gott!*"

"Yep."

In English, Liam again whispered, "Oh, my God. This is impossible. Isn't it?"

Charlie shrugged. He nodded at the leather tube sitting beside their dishes. "What else did the witch give you?"

Liam reached for the blue leather tubular box, disliking the faint tremble he spied in his fingers. He hastily picked it up and untied the leather thong holding the flap shut. He flipped it open. A piece of paper fell out. Charlie saved it from going into the stew. He read it aloud.

"'Open at *midnight* exactly on Christmas Eve. No earlier. No later.'" Charlie handed the paper back. "What's in there?"

Liam turned the box around and tipped it so his friend could look inside.

"A Christmas cracker?"

"That's what it looks like."

Liam lifted the delicate object out of its box and set it on the table.

"Black?"

"I know. I've never seen black paper used before," Liam acknowledged. "It looks homemade."

He touched the dusting of gold sparkles on the black crêpe paper ruffles. He tilted the cracker this way and that to check if the snapper was in place. Sure enough, two thin cardboard strips stuck out of the pinch point of the ruffles. A band of gold and black glossy paper wrapped the tube part of the cracker. Tiny gold silk poinsettias, bits of fake greenery and a short length of gold beads decorated the center of the tube, glued onto the glossy paper. Liam shook it and heard the rattle of the prizes inside. *What could be inside that makes it so heavy?*

"It's beautiful," Liam breathed.

"Kinda creepy."

Liam's brows drew together. "No. Why?"

His friend jabbed his thumb at his own chest. "Charlie Early."

"So?"

"I'm related to Biddy Early. Sure of it. Ireland's most famous witch."

"You're superstitious? Fey? Since when?"

"Since always. You never noticed."

Liam grunted. "We could pull it now and see what happens," he suggested, holding out one end to Charlie.

"Oh, no," he said, folding his arms and leaning back, his blue eyes wide and alarmed. "Follow the directions. Anything might happen if we pull it now."

"But I'll be alone in the woods on Christmas Eve. Who will pull the other end?"

Charlie pointed at Liam's chest. "Only way."

Liam scowled and stared down at the black and gold Christmas cracker.

"Put it away," Charlie ordered, picking up his spoon and

addressing the remains of his stew.

"And if something happens to me out in the woods?" Liam asked, placing the cracker in its tubular home. *What could happen? I'm being foolish.*

"*I'll blame the witch,*" Charlie said in German.

Liam cursed in the same language. "*Fettarsch!*"

Charlie choked on his bite of bannock, spewing bits of the biscuit onto the table.

Chapter Two

Silje leapt over a huge, fallen tree. Her feet failed to find purchase on the slippery layer of wet leaves and slid out from under her. She fell on her backside and rolled into the hollow beneath the trunk. Winded, Silje huddled in a ball, shuddering in reaction to the pain in her arse. The *Skræling* warriors could only be moments behind her.

Did they see me fall?

The dry forest litter beneath the shelter of the logs rustled with every twitch. Carefully, cautious of the noise her movements made, Silje eased piles of dead leaves and twigs into the opening to the hollow, praying that the heap would look natural. Next she examined her hiding place and discovered that the hollow deepened closer to the roots. She scooted in that direction, kicking debris behind her, loosely filling the gap beyond her feet. Soon she was as hidden as it was possible to be.

Calm yourself. Slow your breathing. Be still.

Her dry mouth cried out for moisture but she'd long since dropped her water skin. She discovered a patch of thick moss and tore a handful from the dead log. She held it over her mouth and squeezed a dribble of liquid onto her tongue. The relief was instant and most welcome. She tucked her cold hands into her armpits and lay perfectly still. Of one thing she was grateful—these warriors had not brought their dogs on the hunt.

* * *

Charlie dropped Liam and his supplies at the side of the road near the faint path into the gloomy woods. Early morning ground mist wound through the mixed forest of evergreen and naked deciduous trees. The sun, a pale circle hiding behind a thin layer of clouds, did little to brighten the day.

"So you brought your sword," Charlie said, standing

beside his friend.

"There was a spot for it on the belt," Liam said, shrugging, patting the sword hilt and the leather-bound axe head.

He wore his hand-forged knife in a rawhide chest scabbard. He swung the woven basket pack onto his back and adjusted the fur-lined cloak beneath it. The bear-skin sleeping bag, tied onto the top of the *neverkont,* stuck out on both sides and provided a sort of head rest.

Grimacing, he said, "I'm going to have to get the hang of this...this cloak. Really, it's little more than a blanket thrown across my shoulders."

"Yep," Charlie said, grinning widely and chuckling.

"You're making fun of me, aren't you?"

"Little bit." Charlie flicked the three-inch long safety pin holding the cloak closed. "Got that off of a kilt?"

"Yes, as a matter of fact," Liam said, refusing to be embarrassed about it. "I don't know why I didn't think to buy a proper brooch yesterday."

"I'm surprised the witch didn't slip one into the pile."

Liam's mouth twisted into a lopsided smile. "So am I."

"Warm enough? Got gloves?"

"Sure." Liam glanced up at the sky and around at the lonely stretch of back road. "Time for me to go. I'll meet you here in two weeks. At noon."

"Do you have your phone?"

"No, no phone. No electronic devices." He held up his arm, displaying his watch. "Only my watch. That's it. Oh, and a compass."

"What if you find something?"

"I have my sketchpad if—no, *when* I find something."

"Christmas cracker?" Charlie asked, his right eyebrow quirking up.

"Yes." He and Charlie slapped each other on the arms. "Have a good Christmas."

"You too."

Liam crossed the verge and bounded out of the dip, walking on the barely-there path leading into the forest. As he reached the tree boundary, Charlie called to him.

"Wait!"

Liam turned around and caught Charlie snapping a picture of him with his phone.

"In case I never see you again!" his friend called. Then his expression lost its grin and he took an impulsive step forward. "Liam!"

"Now you're just trying to spook me!" Liam called back, shaking his head. He raised a hand in farewell and plunged into the gloom of the woods.

Three hours later, Liam found an excellent spot to camp next to a break in the forest cover and near a fast-running brook. A butternut tree grew next to the clearing amongst a stand of trembling aspen. The natural extracts from the butternut tree roots discouraged all sorts of plants from growing near it, creating a nicely cleared spot around it. He used his folding shovel to clear the ground of sticky fallen nuts that were not, strictly speaking, directly beneath the tree. Twigs and rotting leaves joined the growing pile. Once satisfied, Liam built a rough lean-to between two slender aspens. He crossed the clearing to a stand of fir and cedar trees, collecting boughs for a mattress. On his second trip across the clearing, he stumbled into a depression in the dead grass. He grunted and fell to one knee, dropping his armload of boughs.

"Damn," he muttered, steadying himself with both hands on the ground.

He winced. Something poked into his left palm. Liam lifted his hand and examined the spot where it had been. *Is there something there? A nail, perhaps? Or just a pointy rock?* He parted the grass and leaned over to look.

And stopped breathing.

He blinked and dropped to the ground, laying full length upon the damp grass so he could examine his find at eye level. A rusted dome shape, approximately six inches across, stuck out of the ground at an angle.

This could be it! Maybe. Maybe. Don't get ahead of

yourself. Get your tools and sketchpad.

Liam leapt up and ran across the clearing to where his woven *neverkont* sat beneath his shelter. He reached inside and drew out a cotton sack containing a sketchpad, a pencil, a small trowel—handmade by him—a boar-bristle brush, and a wooden metric ruler. Back beside his find, he flung himself down on his belly and set to work.

After an hour of painstaking excavation, he uncovered the domed boss of a shield. The boss protected the spot where the bearer's hand gripped the shield. Was it a Viking shield? The shape was not atypical of a Viking iron boss.

Liam measured the encircling up-stand directly off of the flange. "Ten millimeters," he whispered to himself and made a note on the sketch. He hummed a happy few notes while he measured a twelve millimeter knob decorating the top of the dome. He noted this then paused to check over his sketch and compare it to the original. Mumbling under his breath, he added a further comment to the page. "The 'neck' of this boss shape might have been designed to capture...uh...to capture the edge of a sword. The shield bearer could then turn the sword aside."

"Could this...could this be from the Vendel period?" he whispered, hearing the awe in his voice. "No, impossible. The Vendel period predates the Viking Age." He measured and sketched and measured some more, brushing dirt away with the skill of an artisan. "But that would be something...to find...never mind. Stick with what you know, O'Brien," he scoffed. Until it could be carbon dated, Liam wouldn't be certain of anything.

There appeared to be no remains of the wood part of the shield and no sign of the iron strapping that was used to hold the wood together. Though not all shields used iron strapping, its lack seemed suspect to Liam.

Maybe someone found the boss somewhere else and then lost it here. A child playing in the woods?

Liam took a deep breath through his nose, held it and then released it slowly. He refused to be discouraged. Of course, he would have preferred to find evidence of the entire shield, but he remained elated at this find. He frowned. *Yes, what luck to find it on my first day. Hmm. That old Aunty. They'd joked that she was a witch, but they didn't really exist, did they?* Liam listened to his twitching bones and accepted this gift.

He snapped the sketchbook shut, shoved it into the bag and gently, oh so gently, used the trowel to lever the iron boss off of the mound of dirt beneath it.

"Don't fall apart, don't fall apart," he whispered, ignoring the cold breeze blowing across the clearing and the gathering shadows of dusk.

It came up in one piece and Liam sighed in relief. He wrapped the precious object in a clean linen square and carried it across to his shelter. He set it to one side and stared down at it until he realized he could hardly see it.

"Crap," he said and turned to squat beside his prepared fire to light it. Several scrapings at the flint later and a flame appeared in the fine dry tinder beneath the tee-pee wood construction above it. As soon as he was certain the fire wouldn't go out, he hurried across the clearing to collect the pile of boughs he'd left beside the find. He layered some of these over the top of his deadfall lean-to and used the rest for a mattress.

* * *

Silje held her breath and froze. She imagined she was home, far away on the northern tip of the new island where her clan had come to fish and to collect wood for making boats.

I am not here. I am not here. You will not find me.

The three *Skrælingjar* warriors moved through the woods, almost silent. She could not see from her hiding space, only strain to hear the mark of their passage. Like her, they bounded over the fallen tree, landing with whispered slaps on the damp ground.

Do not stop. Go on. Go on. I am far from here. Go. Go.

But they didn't go.

Silje silently curled into a ball, deep within the hollow beneath the tree roots. She heard mutterings that she did not understand and then spears thrust through the opening into the space where she'd been. They poked and prodded and one even broke through the pile of debris she'd kicked into place with her feet. Yet they could not find her where she lay within the embrace of the ancient tree.

The spears disappeared.

More mutterings.

Go, she cried silently, refusing to shift her cramped body, refusing to shiver or attempt to bolt. She kept her hand clenched around her knife. *I'm like a cornered wolverine. Do not find me or I will rip and tear you apart. Go!*

* * *

Liam sat cross-legged on his bed of boughs and bear-fur sleeping bag before his crackling fire. The tubular box containing the Christmas cracker sat on his lap. He looked at his watch where it rested on a flat rock beside him next to his compass. The reflection of the flames danced across its surface. 11:59. *Almost midnight.* He undid the thong tie and flipped back the leather lid, exposing the cracker. He tipped it into his hand and set the box aside. The sparkles on its surface gleamed. He wished he'd brought a modern lamp or a flashlight. The dark of the woods was very dark indeed. His only additional light came from a candle inside a folding tin and glass lamp. The lamp door stood open. Inside, three of the glass sides reflected the light back at him.

The watch chimed.

Midnight.

Liam's heart pounded and his breath came in puffs of cold mist. He clasped one slender cardboard end of the snapper in his left hand and the other in his right.

"Here goes," he murmured.

And pulled.

The sound of the snap reverberated through the cold night air. It was the loudest snap he'd ever heard. Usually, the snap was no louder than a cap gun where a miniscule amount of gunpowder, when struck, created the snap. This sounded like a fire cracker exploding. Yet, the homemade cracker was neither burnt nor exploded.

"Bloody hell," he whispered, shaking his head and knuckling his ear.

Liam pulled off one of the ruffles and pried open the crêpe paper folded over one end of the tube. He poured the contents out onto the bear fur, expecting to find a candy treat, a motto or joke, a simple toy prize and a tissue paper crown. The candy was there—a bittersweet horehound lozenge inside a screw of wax paper. Liam opened it and popped it in his mouth. He'd always liked the taste of these medicinal lozenges, purportedly excellent for sore throats. It took him back to his childhood when his Mi'kmaq grandmother used to make her own.

Liam frowned down at the pile of prizes. He set the remains of the cracker next to the items and knew there was no way that this collection of things could fit inside it. There was a bone flute four inches longer than the tube! And a leather sack of Norse gold coins. And a penannular brooch—an almost closed ring of twisted silver. The long pin, sticking past the ring by about an inch, was not fixed, but rotated about the ring. Liam chuckled. Here was the missing brooch. After examining it closely in the candlelight, Liam measured it against the diameter of the tube. It would not, *could not* fit. The brooch had to be three inches across, more than twice the diameter of the cracker.

"Damn," he whispered. "It's like a bloody T.A.R.D.I.S., bigger on the inside. It's impossible. Who was that old woman?"

He picked up the last items, a hand-woven scarf and a Hardanger embroidered handkerchief.

"It would be a shame to use this," he muttered, shrugged, and tucked the handkerchief inside the cuff of his tunic. He folded the scarf and set it aside.

The motto lay on the fur. He unfolded the slip of paper and examined the runes. After a moment, he read aloud, "He hath need of his wits who wanders wide."

Liam couldn't very well argue with that sentiment. *Merry Christmas to me,* he thought, and gathered up his prizes. He put the brooch, scarf and money bag in the *neverkont*. He collected the cracker debris and almost threw it in the fire. At the last second, he changed his mind and replaced it in the leather tubular box. He put that back in the pack. Liam held the simple bone flute on his palm. He'd learned to play the recorder from his mother who'd been taught it in school just like everyone else of her generation.

Setting the mouth end to his lips, he positioned his fingers over the holes and blew. A clear, sweet note emerged. He smiled and settled down to play a scale. Then, in memory of his mother, he played *Au Claire de la Lune*, her first learned piece. Quiet pleasure surged through him. In his mind's eye, he pictured his dear mother sitting in the kitchen and playing the plastic flute she'd found at a thrift store. Then she'd handed it to him and placed his little fingers over the holes. She'd passed away a few years before of breast cancer. Liam paused between tunes to clear his tight throat.

* * *

Silje stirred and awoke. She'd fallen asleep in dread of being found by the *Skræling* warriors. She blinked rapidly, taking in shallow breaths as she oriented herself. She could not even see her hand right before her face.

How long have I slept?

She shivered. The coolness of day had succumbed to frigid night air. It was time to climb out and see if she could make her way back to the camp and the ships. *What if they were driven off? What if I am alone in this wild land full of strange warriors?* She shoved the urge to panic beneath her spine where it belonged. *If I want to be a shield-maiden, I cannot act like a mouse.* Silje managed to scoot herself around so she could wiggle away from the roots toward the opening. She paused for many long moments and listened. She could hear nothing and the region felt...empty.

Silje brushed the forest detritus off her tunic, jerkin, and trousers as soon as she stood. The night wasn't quite so dark out from beneath the fallen tree trunk. The glow of a full moon sifted through the canopy, dappling the forest floor with slices of silvery light. She climbed over the log, heading back the way she'd come, too cold and frightened to stay put until a search party found her.

And then she heard it.

Music. How? Who? It was a flute, not the drums of the *Skrælingjar*. She paused and rested a hand against a tree. A troll to lure her into his trap? In spite of her conversion to the Christian faith, she couldn't put off the superstitions of her people. They were ingrained in her and as much a part of her life as the new teachings strove to be.

Silje almost retreated but then she smelled it. Wood smoke. The beckoning scent of a fire and the warmth it promised propelled Silje on. Fire equaled safety. Whose fire, though? Her fingers, cramped from holding so tightly to the handle of her blade, opened and closed around the length of antler. Only the ring of her thumb and forefinger kept the precious knife from falling.

A howl sounded in the distance. Silje jumped. *Wolves.* Even though the wolves of Vinland seemed timid compared to those back in the land of her childhood, none of her people liked to hear their bone-chilling song in the night. Silje hastened her steps.

A fire will be nice. I prefer the danger of strangers to the ripping and tearing of my flesh by fangs. And if it be trolls? Silje swallowed and tried not to think of that possibility.

Chapter Three

Liam tucked his flute away, added a couple of fat logs to the fire, slipped off his hand-tooled leather boots, his jerkin, his cloak, and wrapped himself up in his bear-fur sleeping bag. He used his arm as a pillow and stared at the dancing flames, mesmerized.

That Aunty. Why do I keep calling her that? A witch? Surely not. Twitching bones were one thing. Pure magic was another. And yet...the iron boss. What was the likelihood that he would find the evidence he sought on the very first day he arrived? He hadn't even started looking. Then again, many archaeological finds occurred simply by accident—a farmer digging in his field, as a for instance, or a goat herder finding the Dead Sea Scrolls. Then, there was the Viking burial site found during some road construction in Dorset.

"Accidents happen," he murmured drowsily, snuggling deeper, plenty warm enough inside the fur. He closed his eyes. "Doesn't have to be magic."

Silje spied the fire through the gaps in the trees and brush. She circled the camp, searching for a sentry and found no one. The flames drew her closer. There appeared to be no signs of trolls—not that she'd ever seen any of these vile creatures but there'd been talk. Ever since she'd changed her faith, she'd been extra wary as everyone knew that trolls hated the smell of Christians. And church bells. *Fool, there are no churches or bells in Vinland.*

Silje inched closer, watching the long form inside his sleeping bag. The form, too large for a female, rolled in his sleep and the fur shifted away from his face. In repose, his features appeared soft and quietly handsome. His strong dark eyebrows drew in over a bold nose and kissable lips.

Kissable lips! Do not think on his lips. Who is he? Why is he here, so far from the shore? Silje examined his features, shifting closer and closer to the welcoming warmth of the fire. She did not recognize him. Could there be another group of Norsemen visiting Vinland, far from their homes?

A twig fell to the ground, drawing her attention. She spun on her feet, her dagger at the ready, searching the woods and clearing. *Who is there? Nothing.* Silje relaxed, lowering her knife hand. She rotated so she could once more look at the strange man.

And then the sight of a sword hilt captured her attention to the exclusion of all else. A belt hung from a broken branch, near to hand. It held both the sword and an axe. The hilt of the sword, bound in leather strapping, graced by a *steel* guard and topped with a curved brass pommel, gleamed in the dancing flames. The weapon called to her as no other. She *knew* this sword would be just the right weight, exactly the correct length, and so precisely balanced that wielding such a blade might bring tears to her eyes.

How is it possible that this…this stranger has my *sword?*

Without more than a quick glance at the sleeping man, Silje approached the belt. She sheathed her knife and slowly drew the sword. It sang from its sheath with whisper soft precision.

"Ah," she breathed, mesmerized by the high sheen on the two-edged blade. She laid it across her palm and examined the weapon with rapt attention. "Such beauty," she murmured, and then hastily checked to see if the man still slept. He hadn't stirred.

Silje picked up the shield that leaned against the base of the tree and eased away, placing one cautious step behind the other. Once in the clearing before the camp, she swung the sword. She entered into a series of thrusting and parrying exercises that she'd only been permitted to practice with the use of a wood sword or with a blade too heavy for her. This blade was a joy to swing. *Those Skrælingjar are most fortunate they didn't meet me with this sword in my hand!*

Liam's brows drew together. His bones itched and he opened his eyes a slit without moving anything else. He almost called out when the stranger pulled forth his sword and turned toward the fire.

A woman? What is a woman dressed like a Viking doing in these woods? One of Charlie's practical jokes?

The woman appeared to be only twenty or so years old. She was tall—maybe only a few inches shorter than he. Her long, golden-blonde hair hung down on either side of her head in three braids, rejoined as one at the bottom by a copper ring-clamp. A stiff brown leather circlet bound her hair in place, crossing her smooth forehead and fastened at the back. Her high, Nordic cheekbones spoke of her ancestry. Charlie had outdone himself. She was beautiful!

She wore a black leather jerkin, lined in gray fur, over a dark-green tunic, embroidered around the collar and wrists. Trousers of warm-brown wool tucked into black leather boots and walnut-brown putties. She leaned over and picked up a shield.

A shield? Where did she get the shield? Did she bring it with her?

After a swift peek at him, the stranger turned away and he risked a glance at the foot of his shelter where he'd left the artifact. The shield boss was gone. *No, surely not. I must have pushed it to one side with my foot.* The woman moved into the moonlight illuminating the clearing. To his immense surprise, she began to thrust and parry, swinging the blade to and fro at imaginary foes. Her beautiful, full mouth split into a grin.

She loves my sword.

Liam began to wonder if she planned to return it.

Time to find out.

Liam sat up. Cold air hit him and he shivered. He reached for his cloak and swung it over his shoulders. His movements alerted the woman and her gaze fixed on him. He was struck again by her Nordic features. Firelight played across strong cheekbones and pale skin. She scowled at him and took a step toward the camp. And then another.

Liam didn't move except to raise one knee so that his arm could rest across it. He didn't want to frighten her. After all, she was the one holding the sword. In three more steps her eye color revealed itself. Blue. Pale, Nordic blue. As he'd expected.

"You like my sword?" he asked, indicating the blade with a negligent wave of his hand.

The woman tilted her head and narrowed her gaze. *"I do not understand your words."*

Liam's mind clicked over and he replied in Norse. Old Norse. "I'm glad you like it. I think it's my best work so far." Liam's thoughts raced. *Old Norse. Not Icelandic Old Norse. More of a Western Old Norse dialect. What is the chance of that? Is this more evidence of Aunty's strange magic?* As much as he wanted to hold onto the idea that Charlie was responsible for this woman's appearance in the woods, Liam couldn't do it. Or could he? Had Charlie found this woman at the fair, someone into cosplay? Someone who could fake it enough to fool him for a while? *It would be just like Charlie, the bastard. A Christmas gift?*

The woman pressed her lips together and eyed him suspiciously. "You made this sword? You are a blacksmith?"

Liam shrugged and nodded. "I made the sword. It took me two weeks." She didn't respond immediately and she didn't look like she was ready to return the weapon to its sheath. She was very convincing. "My name is Liam. Liam O'Brien."

The woman struck her chest with the fist holding the sword hilt and took a step closer to the fire. "I am Silje Petursdotter, Liam, grandson of Brien."

"Please, sit," Liam suggested, waving at the ground. Not many people knew what O' meant in O'Brien. *Interesting. She really knows her stuff.* "You must be cold."

"The warmth of the fire would be most welcome," Silje replied, sitting cross-legged. She set the shield on the ground beside her and rested the sword across her lap. She kept one hand on the hilt while holding the other out to the flames.

"What are you doing out here in the middle of the woods

at night?" Liam asked, then added in English, hoping to trick her into revealing herself: "Without even a cloak to keep you warm?"

She didn't answer his questions. Was that because she didn't want to or because she didn't understand? Both? Instead she sucked in her breath and stared him in the eye.

"How is it that you have a sword that is perfect for me? It slices through the air as though an extension of my arm. What is her name?"

"Her?" Liam asked. He reached over for the woven pack and felt around in it for a leather pouch. He pulled it free, opened it wide, and took out a chunk of beef jerky. "I haven't named it yet." He offered the dried piece of meat to his guest and she almost snatched it out of his hand. *Okay, she's a little bit hungry. Who is this woman? Besides a brilliant actress.* "I've thought and thought but no name has come to me. What do you think? Got any ideas?"

Silje smiled. "Gut Slasher." She gnawed on the meat and looked from him to the sword and back again.

"Really?" Liam's skepticism brought her brows together.

"In truth," she asserted, nodding once. "Gut Slasher."

"King Magnus Barelegs named his sword Legbiter."

She shrugged. "I do not know this king."

Liam raised an eyebrow. Surely a serious Viking cosplayer would know about King Magnus Barelegs. His bones twitched and he sucked in his breath. The family intuition was acting up. The impression he received was that she was the real deal, but he resisted that possibility and his bones didn't like his stubbornness. "Never mind. It doesn't matter. So, Gut Slasher it is." He leaned forward, losing his negligent attitude. "But really, what are you doing out here? Is your camp nearby?"

Silje started to deny it and then thought better of revealing so much to this stranger. Did he hale from the island of Eire as his name suggested? Where was his ship? The rest of his group? Have they all died?

"Has your ship floundered, Liam? Is that what brought you so far from your home?"

"Nay. Charlie brought me," he replied and the puzzlement in his gaze held her own.

Ah but he has a fine set of brown eyes. Odd. It must be the Eire blood in his veins. Silje took another bite of the delicious dried meat and chewed thoughtfully, watching him eat.

"Who is Charlie?" she asked, raising an eyebrow at his confused stare. "You expect me to know this person? Who is he? Or is Charlie a woman?"

Liam swallowed, took a skin and squeezed water into his mouth before handing the skin to her, and then said, "Charlie's male and he's my best friend."

"If he is out in the woods tonight, he must have a mind to the *Skrælingjar* who roam these forests. It is they who drove me from the safety of my camp and into this wild place." Silje squeezed a stream of cold water into her mouth and wished it was ale, though she cast that thought aside. *I must keep my wits about me this night.* "I was gathering nuts in the woods near my camp when they attacked me. I managed to get away—I am very fleet of foot—but they drove me deeper into the forest."

"*Skræling?*"

"Aye. Did you not see them earlier? A band of at least three men chased me. I hid beneath a log until nightfall."

She passed back the water-skin. Liam took it and laid it to one side. He breathed deeply for several moments, causing cold-air steam to spew from his nostrils like a bull ready to charge. *What has raised his ire? It must be the mention of the Skrælingjar.*

"By Odin's missing eye," Liam said, his fists clenched now and resting on the ground beside him. "Did you say *Skræling?*"

"Aye. What is amiss?"

It isn't possible. How can it be? Liam stroked one eyebrow and stared into the glowing coals, reviewing the events of the last two weeks, beginning with the day he'd opened the government letter and found permission to explore this area of the New Brunswick wilderness. He hadn't expected permission to come so quickly. And the apartment had fallen into his lap too. As if...as if...as if a greater power had been at work. Then there'd been the stall where he'd bought all his Viking gear—the stall that had disappeared the moment they'd left it. How was that possible? And what about the speaking in tongues? He'd never learned more than a few phrases and words in German.

She'd said *Skræling*—the Viking name for the native peoples they found in Vinland. He savored the word, pronouncing it in his mind as skreeyling, in a sort of sing-song silent voice that echoed each time he thought it. *Skrælingjar*— the plural form.

The only completely impossible explanation to this situation was that this woman had come forward in time. *Impossible.* Liam caught his breath and stared at the shield. The boss in the center appeared to be exactly like the one he'd found. Yet...yet...the iron was whole and perfect. If Silje was not a cosplayer, if she had indeed come forward in time, surely there would be no shield, only the rusty iron boss he'd found earlier. The shield was whole. It was only whole in the past. His thoughts stuttered and reversed.

Could it be that I'm *the one who's gone through time?*

Wait. Wait! How can I even think such a thing?

The itching of his bones made him shift uneasily. His intuition, or whatever someone else might call it, did not like it when he denied its influence. *But how?* He remembered the bang from pulling the Christmas cracker snap. The tiny snap had sounded like a giant firecracker. Had that been the moment? Liam tensed his jaw. *Magic?*

The construction of the fire shifted, drawing his gaze to Silje, who poked a fresh chunk of wood onto the coals.

"What is amiss?" she repeated, holding his gaze.

I'm going to play along, he thought, taking a deep breath to clear his racing thoughts. *For tonight. Tomorrow, I'll follow the path back to the road and then I'll know for sure. And, when I find the road right where I left it, I'm never going to tell anyone about this momentary diversion into madness. Not even Charlie. No,* especially *not Charlie.*

"As you say, my ship floundered," he said, frowning sadly, improvising on the fly. "We limped ashore." He paused and waved in an easterly direction. "My fellow sailors repaired the hull. While I was exploring, the group was attacked and had to take to the sea to escape. I watched from a bluff, too far away to help."

"They sent their blacksmith to explore?" Silje asked, clearly puzzled. "Surely they had need of your skills during the repair work?"

Liam fell back on the ambiguity of an expressive shrug. "The master carpenter jealously guarded his guild-craft."

"Fool."

Silje's response drew a chuckle from him. "Indeed." He indicated his supplies. "We unloaded the ship to tilt it for the repairs. I thought it easier and safer to carry my gear rather than leave it sitting amongst the tidal pools."

"Good thinking," she said and gazed lovingly down at the sword on her lap. "Elsewise you might have lost Gut Slasher to the *Skrælingjar.* They do not use swords, or any other type of metal craft, but my sword would have been a prize for them."

"*Your* sword?" Liam rumbled, narrowing his gaze. "Are you thinking of taking it from me?"

Silje's hand tightened on the grip and she scowled ferociously at him. "As you see, it is already in my possession. I took the blade easily from you while you slept."

"That is theft. Pure and simple. My belt, my axe, my sword. Clearly." Liam waited for Silje's response, but she wasn't listening to him. Instead, her head was cocked to one side and her eyelids lowered to half-closed. "Look, Silje. You snuck into my camp and—"

"Hold!" she commanded in a hiss, rising to her feet in one swift motion. She snatched up the shield and held it before her, swiveling about, searching the woods around them. "Rise and

109

take up your axe, Liam O'Brien, ere we are cut down where we sit."

Chapter Four

Liam didn't move as quickly as his guest and she dove for the belt. She lifted it down and threw it at him.

"Rise from the heat of your bed, take up your axe and be ready," she ordered in a quiet snarl. "Do it. Did you think these woods safe?"

Liam shoved back the rest of his bear-skin sleeping bag and yanked on his boots. "There is no one out there who would hurt us."

"I heard the howling of the wolf earlier. And the *Skrælingjar* may yet come upon us."

Liam rose to his feet and unsheathed his Viking axe, removing the leather guard that protected the razor sharp steel edge. The haft was short—only thirty-two inches long—indicating that the axe was intended for one-armed use. The fighter would hold his shield in his non-dominant hand and swing the axe with his dominant one. In Liam's case, that meant he used the axe in his right hand. Silje had the shield. He hadn't brought one. Why would he have needed a shield? *The old Aunty...No, I'm going to call her what she is, the old* witch, *didn't sell me a shield either. She told me to bring a sword, but not a shield. Merry bloody Christmas to me.*

"There are no wolves in this land," Liam commented, while obediently grasping his axe to appear that he was ready to use it. He exited his shelter and moved to stand next to her. "And whichever *Skrælingjar* that live in this area have long since gone to sleep. So have the bears."

Silje scoffed in a grim whisper. "And trolls? Are they sleeping too? In the night?"

Liam blinked several times and drew his brows together. *Trolls?* He admired the strength of her acting skills. Silje rolled her sword wrist, making the blade arc in a circle.

"Do you still hear something?" Liam asked, concentrating

on the night sounds.

Silje gave a short shake of her head. Liam pressed his lips together into a thin line and wandered out into the clearing. The full moon illuminated the space and as his eyes adjusted further, he realized he could see the ground.

And he couldn't see where he'd been digging earlier in the day. Cool fire flowed through his veins.

It isn't possible.

Liam examined the clearing again. Was it the same as before he'd pulled the Christmas cracker? Did that clump of evergreens seem larger? He couldn't tell. Not by moonlight anyway. He barely heard Silje's call.

"Come back to the firelight, fool!"

Liam rolled his shoulders. Someone was watching them. He felt it in the itch between his shoulder blades and in the tightening of his stomach muscles. He backed up slowly, his axe at the ready, keenly aware that he carried no shield. Was it a bear? The winter had been so warm this year that he'd heard reports of bears putting off their hibernation. He hefted the light-weight axe, confident in the sharpness of the blade. *Can I kill a bear with only an axe? Could I do it? So up close and personal?*

He'd hunted before. He'd trained in bow hunting in Denmark during a study-abroad year. He was accurate. Deer. Elk. Wild grouse. Even moose. He'd never drawn on a bear though. Not that it mattered because he didn't have his hunting bow set—one more thing the witch had neglected to tell him to bring.

Liam backed toward her and Silje moved forward so they stood shoulder to shoulder.

"Someone is coming," she whispered. "Enemy? Or could it be your friends? Have they come back for you?"

"Nay. They wouldn't search in the dark."

She acknowledged the sense in that and opened her mouth to suggest something else when three *Skrælingjar* detached themselves from the shadows and entered the clearing. Her heart leapt into her throat and she trampled on the urge to flee. Now they were two to three. Those were easy odds for a Norse warrior and a shield-maiden. She tightened her grip on the amazing sword and smiled. This time, she had Gut Slasher.

The *Skrælingjar* wore leather leggings and fur cloaks that hung to their knees, tightened around their waists with woven belts. Their raven-black hair blended with the night like evil creatures released from Hel. They each carried a club formed from a sharp stone bound between split wooden hafts. Unaccountably, her companion relaxed his stance.

"Are you mad?" she demanded. "Be on your guard!"

"It'll be all right," he said, smiling at her.

And then he spoke to the *Skrælingjar*, holding his arms wide in welcome. In their own tongue!

"Hale and welcome," Liam said. *The gift of tongues strikes again.* "Welcome to my fire. It is a cold night and all are welcome."

The Mi'kmaq warriors stared at him, their expressions impassive. The one in the middle stepped ahead of the others.

"We have searched for this woman," he said, waving his club at Silje. "Is she your woman?"

Liam remained calm. These must be the men whom Silje claimed had chased her. There was no way Charlie could have planned all of this. There'd been no time. The truth boggled his mind. He had to stiffen his suddenly weak knees and control his impulse to laugh hysterically.

I'm in the past.

I'm in the past.

Damn, damn, damn.

The Mi'kmaq warrior waited patiently for his answer. Liam pulled himself together and replied the only way he could, the only sensible way. "Yes. She is my woman. Why were you searching for her?"

"She is your *wife?*" the first warrior repeated, ignoring the question.

"As I said."

The younger warrior to the speaker's left whispered something in his ear. The speaker stared at Silje, narrowing his eyes ever so slightly.

"Are you this man's wife?" he asked.

Silje curled her lip and muttered, "What did he say?"

Liam switched languages. In a calm voice, he explained. "They want to know if you are my wife." She shifted from one foot to the other and her grip on the sword tightened. She hadn't taken her gaze off the three warriors but he had the distinct impression that she was ready to kill *him* instead. "You can nod, if you don't want to speak. That should be sufficient proof that I'm telling the truth."

"We should just kill them. Why are we wasting time with talk?" she hissed.

"*That* should make everything right and tight," Liam replied, a strong sarcastic edge to his words. "The entire tribe would be upon us or your people if these men don't return. Come on, how hard can it be to just nod. If we're lucky we can get out of this mess without any further trouble."

Silje's whole body appeared tense and ready to spring. However, before the three warriors reacted to her hesitation, she gave a sharp nod.

"There," Liam said to the Mi'kmaq speaker, sighing inwardly with relief. "She has agreed. We are married."

Seemingly satisfied, the younger warrior stepped back into place.

"You are both," the speaker pointed again with his club to Silje and then to Liam, "with the other tall men who come from across the sea? They steal our food and take our trees."

Liam thought furiously and finally said, "Aye, we are with them. There are plenty of trees and provisions for all. Is that why you chased my woman? Because she was collecting nuts without your permission?"

"It is so."

Liam turned to Silje and said in Old Norse, "Drop the sword and shield, kneel on the ground, and bow to these men."

Silje's eyes blazed. "I will *not*."

"You picked their nuts without permission," Liam explained. "Unless you want them to come upon us in our sleep and kill us, you must apologize. Kneel. Please."

Silje's nostrils flared. Liam looked back at the Mi'kmaq and shrugged. In their language he said, "My wife is new to her duties. She should have been married younger but her father is old and her mother is dead so she had much power in their wigwam. She learned to fight and to hunt because she has no brothers. And so, she has little humility."

The eldest of the three cocked an eyebrow and said, "You should beat her."

Liam touched his chest. "Your advice is sound, brother, but she is close to my heart." He turned his head and glared at Silje. She glared back. Then, while still glowering, and without dropping either the shield or the sword, she lowered herself to one knee. Immediately, she stood again, her chin raised and her lips hard.

"She will give you trouble, that one," the elder Mi'kmaq said, a smile barely creeping out.

"There is truth in what you say, but think of what sons she will give me," Liam replied, grinning broadly. "They will be fierce warriors indeed."

The Mi'kmaq smiled. The first one spoke. "How is it that you speak the proper language so well?"

Liam drew on the truth. "My grandmother was of your people. She taught me your tongue."

This news arrested the warriors. Did they believe him?

"What was her name?" the elder warrior asked.

"My grandfather called her Anna."

"I do not know this name," the elder said, his suspicion clear.

Now Liam had to lie. Again. His conscious pricked him but he ignored it. "She was taken as a young girl while fishing from the rocks further along the coast. A violent wave came and swept her out to sea. She claimed that the creator, *Glooscap*, lifted her in his mighty hand and placed her in my grandfather's lap. He sailed back to his homeland and took her as his wife."

The three warriors looked at each other and while their expressions gave little away, they seemed to be impressed with his story.

"Why are you here?" the speaker asked. "So far from your family?"

Liam placed his hand on Silje's shoulder. "Our binding is fresh. It is the custom of our people for the new couple to be apart for a night or two so they might find their way together."

"It is a good custom." The speaker tipped his head to one side in a sort of half-nod. "We will watch over you so your...sleep...will be undisturbed. There are wolves and bears and cougars abroad tonight."

"And tomorrow, we will walk with you on your journey back to your family so you will not lose your way in *our* forests," the elder Mi'kmaq warrior said.

Without waiting for a response, they faded into the woods, leaving Liam alone with Silje. He turned to her and said, "They're watching us. I'm sorry, but I had to tell them that we're together. You needed to have a protector. If they thought you were free, they might have tried to take you. And, I'm sorry...it's madness, I know, but it's important that you walk behind me back to the fire."

"*Behind* you?" Silje hissed, her eyes wide and furious. "*Behind* you like a dog following its master?"

Liam's insides tensed. In a slow, methodical voice, he replied. "Aye. Like...a...wife."

A *wife*. Silje swayed on her feet. Her companion—her *husband* took gross advantage and set out for his camp, leaving her in the middle of the clearing, her heart pounding and her chest rising and falling like bellows at a forge fire.

A wife.

She'd never wanted to be a wife. Not ever. How could she be a shield-maiden and a wife? There would be no time to train. Housework and children would fill her hours. She thought furiously. No one need ever know. It had been a trick, merely, to fool the *Skrælingjar*. The declaration had not been before her family or her village. There'd been no priest.

Silje jogged after the strange man who was turning her life upside down. When she reached him, she stood on one side of the glowing embers while he squatted on the other side, adding fresh wood to the fire.

"We are *not* married," she insisted.

Liam glanced up at her. "They must think we are. I will not have my tale found out." He turned on his heels and straightened the bear fur. "I'm tired. You must be too after the day you've had. Here, have some more dried meat," he said, tossing the bag at her feet. "I expect you're still hungry."

Silje stood undecided. The discomfort of her extreme frown exhausted her. Though she'd slept earlier beneath the log, the pull of sleep ground her resistance down. There was no certain way to return to her fellow Norsemen, who must be looking for her. Or were they? She brushed her forehead with the back of her wrist. *Fool. Of course they are looking for me. I am their chieftain's daughter.*

Liam removed his cloak, folded it into a pillow long enough for two, and settled himself on the open sleeping bag. He removed his boots, set them to one side, and laid facing the fire, one arm under his head and the bear fur folded over him. He'd left space for her. *Does he expect me to share his bed?* Silje's heart stuttered. She'd never shared any man's bed. She shivered and sunk to her knees beside the fire.

"I would prefer that you sheath the sword," he said, catching her gaze. Then he sighed. "If it pleases you, the sword is yours. You seem to know how to use it better than I do in any case."

Silje rose and hastened over to where his belt lay over the gathered wood. She undid her own belt and then removed the frog and sheath from his. In a trice the sword was in its sheath and the frog to hold the sheath had been threaded onto her belt. *My own sword. At last.* She carried her belt over to the fire, scooped up the bag of dried meat and hesitated.

"If we are to maintain the illusion of being married, then

you must sleep with me," the man said and then, in a most calm, reasonable voice, he added, "Besides, you will be cold if you do not."

"I...I could use your cloak," Silje said, despising the note of entreaty she heard in her voice.

"You cannot use my cloak," Liam said. He patted the fur in front of him. "Come, sit near and learn to be comfortable with me while you eat."

Silje stared into his lovely brown eyes. The light of silent laughter entered their depths.

"You are not afraid of me are you?"

She glowered at him and sat down beneath the lean-to roof so that her backside rested against his stomach.

"Do not be alarmed," he dared to say before encircling her waist with his arm. "I am merely playing a part. Set your sword to one side and eat something."

Silje's stomach muscles contracted. The strength of his arm, warm from being beneath the fur, pleased her more than she would admit. She set the belt beside her near to hand and opened the bag. She chose a large piece of dried meat.

"What manner of animal flesh is this?" she asked, then gnawed off a piece. "It is most tasty."

"Thank you. I made it myself. Some of it is beef and some of it is moose. My friend Charlie...uh..." he paused and sighed. "We used to hunt together."

"Why are you sad?" Silje asked, reaching for the water skin and half-turning toward him. "Is Charlie dead?"

"Well, not exactly. But I don't expect I will ever see him again."

"Because your people left you here?"

"Aye."

Silje squirted water in her mouth and set the skin aside. She rested one hand on his arm in comfort and continued to eat. Sitting this close to a man not of her family confused her. If...*if*...she ever wanted to marry—which she wouldn't, not ever—then this was the type of man she'd want. Strong. Considerate. Intelligent enough to know when not to fight.

Very comely. She felt a blush heat her face and told herself it was the fire.

Liam noticed the blush. Silje was beautiful and feisty. He liked her and he could not deny the attraction between them. He had to find a place with her people. If he was left here, he would be alone with the Mi'kmaq and as fascinating as that might be, he'd rather be part of the Norse culture, the culture he'd studied for the last ten years. All of his adult life, in fact. Silje was his way in. She might claim that their union did not exist but he knew they'd satisfied the letter of the law at least. They'd declared themselves before others and he'd given her a bride gift. The sword. Gut Slasher. As her husband, he would be accepted into the clan and he wouldn't be left behind.

His *wife* finished eating. He took the bag of jerky from her and reached over to put it away in his *neverkont*. Recalling the handkerchief he'd been given in the Christmas cracker, Liam tugged it out from his sleeve and handed it to Silje. She dampened it and wiped her face and hands. She laid the cloth down on a fresh log near the fire to dry. She hung her leather jerkin on one of the lean-to support poles. Though she hesitated, she finally placed her head upon the cloak-pillow beside him and wriggled her legs into the bear-fur bag. She put one hand under her cheek and kept the other on the sword sheath.

Liam smiled and pulled her back against him, then enveloped them both in fur. Gradually, her stiff body relaxed.

"Warm enough?"

"Aye."

"Comfortable?"

She took a moment to reply, then said, "Aye."

"Even though you're still wearing your knife?"

Silje removed the blade and tucked it under the bear skin.

"That's better. Uh, Silje?"

"Aye?"

"Roll over and look at me, please."

He saw the shadows of her furrowed brow when she

119

turned around. Her body had stiffened again.

"What is it, Liam?"

"We have to make love."

Chapter Five

Silje reared back, scrambling to get away from this trickster, searching beneath the fur for her knife. Before she could grasp it, his arms tightened like iron bands around her. She pushed against his chest and tried to knee him in the groin. He grunted and wrapped a leg around hers, trapping her body against his.

"Hush, Silje."

She barred her teeth and went for his neck.

"Whoa," he said, rolling them over so he pressed her into the ground with his weight. "You don't understand. Please don't be afraid of me. I would not—"

"I fear no man," she growled, squirming mightily. "Let me up."

"Nay, I will not," Liam responded, blinking down at her. "The *Skrælingjar* are watching. We must make them think we're making love."

Silje stilled. "A pretence?"

"Aye. A pretence," Liam said, grinning down at her. "Except for kissing."

Silje glared. "Kissing?"

"We can pretend to make love, but fake kissing would just look silly."

And then he proceeded to purse his lips and groan and move his head back and forth, smacking his lips and looking altogether ridiculous.

Silje's anger abated and she couldn't contain a giggle. He laughed and he looked so handsome she caught her breath. Perhaps there would be no harm in a few kisses. He must have sensed her change of heart because he rested the weight of his body on his elbows and gently captured the sides of her head between his large hands.

"Your beauty warms my soul," he whispered.

She felt his breath against her skin right before his mouth touched hers. His lips moved across her lips, tasting, teasing, and learning their shape. A moan sounded and she needed a moment to realize the moan had come from her.

Oh, so this is kissing. It is most pleasant.

Silje touched his cheek, felt the tickle of his beard against her palm, and thrilled to the power of the moment. His lips moved from her mouth to the arc of her cheek and then to the curve of her neck. His breath against her skin sent hot shivers through her body. She craned her head to the side so he might reach every inch of exposed flesh.

"Your skin is so soft," Liam breathed. "I love touching it."

Silje didn't know what to say. Should she thank him? Her thoughts twirled in her head like a will-o-wisp.

"Kiss me again?" she asked.

"Gladly."

Liam's lips descended and this time they weren't quite so gentle. This time he captured her lips and plundered them. He tugged at her lower lip with his teeth and slanted his mouth over hers. Silje gasped in surprised delight and his tongue swept inside. She curved her body against his and clutched at his shoulders.

What sort of sorcery is this? What is he doing to me?

Silje deliberately rubbed her tongue against his and his moan of pleasure triggered a sense of power she'd never known before. Her delight increased three fold. She tugged at his hair, pulling him closer, keeping him from drawing away. He tasted delicious and their tongues warred and danced together. At last Liam tore his mouth away and both panted for breath, groaning softly.

"Again," Silje whispered.

Liam shook his head and placed his cheek against hers. His chest heaved as though he rowed across a fjord. He stroked her hair and his fingertips caressed her other cheek. Shivery tingles dashed down her spine.

"Nay, we...must not," Liam murmured between breaths. "Else we will not be *pretending* to make love tonight."

Disappointment, sharp and aching swept over her. Then came shame. She had begged him to kiss her again—a man she had only met a scarce time ago. Silje tried to roll away from him but he held her still.

Liam attempted to breathe steadily in order to calm his racing heart. Silje belonged in his arms. She fit perfectly. Her soft lips beckoned him to taste her again. He wanted to hold her close and never let her go. She struggled, however, to be let free. It was imperative to their deception that he keep her next to him. He sought to calm her with the truth.

"Your kisses make me drunk with longing," he admitted in a faint pant of air into the curve of her flawless ear. Silje stopped struggling. He drew back and traced the line of her eyebrows with his thumbs. "Did you enjoy my kisses?"

Silje shrugged and wouldn't meet his eyes. Liam released a great rumbling laugh that rolled across the clearing. He hugged her close.

He relaxed his grip and looked into her eyes. "You know, it just now occurred to me that you might already be married. Are you?"

"Nay," the Norse maiden said, almost choking on the word. Her lips pressed tight together as though she kept them from blurting out any further information.

"Hmm," he said. "Have you ever...?"

Silje shook her head in quick jerky motions and color flooded her cheeks.

"I see. It's nothing to be ashamed of, you know," Liam said. He felt her shrug. He kissed the tip of her nose. He couldn't help himself. Normally valiant and feisty, Silje's embarrassment only made her more adorable. Mind you, she might become deadly if he laughed at her discomfiture. "The reason I ask is that I need to know if you know what a man and woman...uh...well..."

"Aye. I am no idiot, Liam O'Brien. I am two and twenty and I know what passes between a man and a woman beneath the furs in the longhouse."

Now she sounded affronted. Liam smiled and nodded. "Good. So, you know what we will have to pretend to be doing."

"Aye. I know. Proceed with haste," Silje exclaimed, grabbing his shoulders and squeezing. "I have heard that the *Skrælingjar* take their women from behind, like dogs. Is this true? Should we pretend this method?"

Liam opened his eyes wide. "I...I can't say if that is their preference. Uh, that method would be difficult to hide—I mean the covers would fall off and they would see that we were pretending."

Silje nodded. "Then?"

Liam grinned and kissed her quickly. "I like you very much," he declared. Before she could respond, he lifted one of her legs and placed it at his waist. "Wrap your legs around my middle. That will keep your...your pelvis away from...Uh, never mind. Just wrap your...that's right." Liam closed his eyes and shuddered inwardly. All the kissing and hugging and struggling and more kissing and hugging had left him in no very comfortable condition.

"Should I grunt? I have heard couples grunting," Silje assured him. Then, with a twisted grin, she added, "Aye, and moaning."

Liam rested his forehead against hers and gave a ragged chuckle. "This is the oddest thing I have ever done."

"In truth?"

"Aye. Okay, one time I filled a man's private chamber with goats."

Silje frowned. "Whyfor?"

"I was young and I did it for a wager." Liam dug his knees into the fur-bow mattress and thrust his hips forward. His movements forced a rush of air out of Silje and she grunted. She blinked and gave a little giggle. Liam continued his account to keep his mind off of his actions. "There were forty-one goats. Big ones, small ones, baby ones."

Silje gasped at his next thrust. "Why goats?"

"The man liked to tell the tale of the Three Billy Goats

Gruff. He had a...grunt...pointed beard...pant...that looked like a goat's."

Silje squeezed her legs around his waist and whispered, "Why is your face screwed up like that?"

"I'm trying to look as if I'm in the throes of passion."

"Oh."

"You be the troll and I'll be the goats," Liam said, needing further diversion to keep his passions under control. "I'm going to lean on my hands, so hold the bear skin around us."

Silje grabbed hold of the corner of the bear skin and kept it covering them when Liam placed one hand on either side of her shoulders and levered himself up. Her hips followed and she gave an experimental groan. His hips thrust toward her and she felt the hard length of him against her bottom.

"Ohhhh," she gasped, staring at Liam's startled expression. He bit his lip and fell down onto his elbows again.

"Bad idea, bad idea," he muttered. He swallowed hard. "Now. The tale. Uh, it begins, *trip trap, trip trap.*"

"What is that?" Silje asked, trying to use the tale to distract her. Liam's warmth, his movement against her, the strain readily apparent on his face, all combined to make her want to touch him all over. To remove his tunic and to pull his hips against hers. *This is pretence. Only pretence.* "Trip trap?"

Liam shuddered. "It's the sound of the youngest Gruff's hooves on the bridge...groan..." He took several deep breaths. "Now it's your turn. You're the troll, remember?"

"Liam?"

"Aye?"

"I can take no more of this pretence. Can we not be at an end?"

"Um...Um...aye. Aye," he said, thrusting again. "Pinch me."

"What say you?"

"Pinch me. Hard."

"Why? I understand not."

"To distract me," Liam said through his gritting teeth. "I

have to...uh...just do it, please."

Silje didn't understand but she obediently shoved both hands into his tunic opening, grabbed a handful of chest hair with one hand and his nipple with the other. She tugged with all her might on his hair and twisted his nipple violently. Liam stiffened, shouted, and jerked against her. Not wanting to be left out, Silje cried out the way she'd heard others in the longhouse.

Liam collapsed over her, burying his face in her neck. She lowered her legs and took his weight, thrilling to it. She could feel his hard length against her thighs and knew he'd found no release in their pretence. In spite of his obvious need, Liam hadn't taken advantage of their situation. Instead, he rolled off her and shook with silent laughter. Silje smiled in response, rising on one elbow so she could bend over him.

"Was that sufficient, do you think?" she asked and chuckled when he covered his eyes with one forearm. His smile pulled his cheek muscles taut.

"You didn't get to play the troll under the bridge," Liam said.

"Another time."

"If we have to do that again I think it will kill me," Liam replied. He sighed and chuckled.

She said nothing and after a moment he lifted his arm and gazed at her, a small frown creasing his brow.

"Are you all right?"

"Aye." Silje affected a huge exhausted sigh—the fiction took no effort for she *was* exhausted. She rolled over and snuggled against the cloak-pillow, one hand beneath her cheek and the other tucked between her legs.

Liam rolled toward her, took her spare hand, entwined it with his between her breasts and embraced her from behind. He still wanted her yet he had great restraint. He might not be a warrior but he had strength she could admire. Other maidens would admire him as well. Her teeth clenched at the thought. There were a set of twins—with only fifteen years—back in the main camp who would want Liam for one of them. She had twenty and two years—too old for most men to crave even if she was the chieftain's daughter.

"Relax," Liam murmured. "Sleep."

"The fire is dying. Wolves might come."

He released her hand and leaned over her. He rolled a fat log onto the coals and settled back, taking her hand again.

"That should do for a while," he said, sighing. "Tomorrow will come soon enough and then we will have to return to your family and face the music."

"Face the music?"

"Your fellow Norsemen must have been searching for you," he suggested, easing more deeply beneath the bear-fur. "They will be pleased to see you safe."

Will they? Her uncle led this expedition and he would not be best pleased that she'd disappeared. She expected he thought she'd been willful again and became lost in the forest due to her inability to follow simple orders. She pressed her lips together. No doubt he would think it a good thing she had to spend a night away from the group in the dark of the forest. Perhaps he thought she would return with new respect for his direction.

Liam's chest rose and fell in a steady rhythm. His heart beat a strong cadence against her back. In truth, she'd never felt more safe. She wondered, now, if the entire day had been directed by fate so she would find herself laying next to her...to her *husband*...a stranger who tugged at her heart with every smile and with each confident movement. They weren't truly married for she'd only nodded as a declaration. Was that sufficient? Was that enough to protect her...man...from the Twins? Would Liam see it as satisfactory, or would he feel trapped by his trick?

Silje closed her eyes and thought on the pretence they had just enacted for the benefit of the watching *Skrælingjar*. A smile curled her lips. Liam had a strong strain of sensible ridiculousness in him that she had not thought to admire in a man. The Three Billy Goats Gruff, indeed. *No doubt he will act out the tale for our children.*

Silje's eyes popped open and her body stiffened.

Wait. Wait. What madness is this? I don't want a husband!

Liam took a deep breath and squeezed her hand. Sleep slurred his words. "All will be..." Sigh. "...all will be well."

Silje relaxed. A tear slipped down her cheek and she couldn't tell if the tear came from sadness, anger, or relief that now she wasn't alone.

Chapter Six

Liam woke first the next morning with the feeling that he was being watched. He opened his eyes a slit. The three Mi'kmaq warriors sat cross-legged on the other side of the fire. The speaker from the night before lifted a wood plank in offering. What looked to be dried cod was piled in the center of the plank.

"Good morning," Liam said to them.

Silje started awake, immediately reaching for the sword lying nearby. He placed a hand on her shoulder.

In Old Norse, he said to Silje, "We have guests. They've brought us some fish for our morning meal."

Silje threw off the bear-fur and grabbed her jerkin for the morning had dawned clear and cold. She shoved her arms through the openings, keeping her cautious gaze on the three warriors.

"I must..." she paused and waved off into the woods behind them.

"I will wait for you to return before I also...uh...retire to the woods."

When she stood she strapped on her belt. She tugged her jerkin into place and stomped off, one hand resting on the sword pommel, the other on her knife.

Liam rose and slipped on his boots. He searched the contents of his woven backpack, found his wooden comb, his small cast-iron Dutch oven, his cotton bags of quick-oats, dried fruit, salt and cinnamon. Beside the jerky, this was all the food left in his pack. His freeze-dried food pouches had disappeared. *This is just great. What if Silje hadn't come along? What if...* He cut off that thought. He'd never had a 'what if' sort of temperament. He looked around for the watch and compass he'd put on a rock before he'd gone to sleep the first time the night before. The rock wasn't there and neither were the watch or compass. Another search of the pack revealed that his toothbrush and toothpaste were gone too. *I'm going to have to find another way to keep my teeth clean. I could use a stick. Better than nothing,* he supposed. *Better than getting a cavity. A cavity?* He gave an inward shudder. *It's too early in the morning to have a thought like that.*

He squirted water into the bottom of the pot and set it on the coals to one side of the fire. He added a pinch of salt and a large pinch of cinnamon to the water, then a handful of diced dried fruits. The smell of the spice perked the interest of the three warriors.

"Cinnamon," Liam said, forced to use English as there was no word in the Mi'kmaq language for it. He held the bag to his nose, sniffed, smiled, and handed the bag to one of the warriors. "Smell it," he said, waving his hand in encouragement.

They obediently sniffed the spice.

"Taste it if you want," Liam said. "It's ground bark."

The elder warrior licked the tip of his finger and dipped it into the brown powder. He tasted the cinnamon and mumbled beneath his breath, nodding to his fellows. He passed the bag on. Each of them partook before handing the bag back to Liam.

The water in the pot started to simmer. Liam scooped out two large handfuls of oats into the pot. He preferred a thick porridge. Porridge for five would use up five days' worth of breakfasts. *Never mind, I won't be camping on my own after today, I hope.* Liam used a spoon of his own making to stir the pot.

Silje returned. Liam gave her the long-handled spoon and headed off into the woods, hoping the stream was right where he'd left it so many hundreds of years in the future. *Hell, I'm probably a thousand years into the past.* He shook his head in amazement, turning his back on the camp, intent on accomplishing his ablutions as quickly as possible.

Silje watched him go. He'd forgotten to take his axe. In what world had he been raised where the need of a weapon did not occupy his thoughts? She looked at the spoon in her hand. *What am I to do with this?* Cooking had never been something she wanted to learn. She'd always known that she would be a shield-maiden when she left her childhood behind. *Married* women, young maids who wished to marry, and thralls cooked. She glanced at the three warriors. They sat perfectly still, their hands on their knees, staring at her. *No help from them.* Silje examined the bubbling pot on the fire. *Stir? I can stir.* She squatted and stuck the spoon in the porridge. Her stomach growled and she decided to take extreme care in stirring the pot so that not a drop slopped out into the coals and so the mixture did not burn. It smelled delicious.

When Liam returned he wasn't wearing his tunic. She swiveled in her crouch and watched him walk bare-chested into the camp. He carried his tunic balled up in one hand, blotting at the water glistening on his skin. His muscles rippled and bunched with each step and she couldn't stop her eyes from widening in sudden female appreciation. Then she frowned. He didn't have a single scar. Hold, there on his lower front, a small straight scar not a finger's length long. If she'd needed any more evidence that he wasn't a warrior, here it was. Unless that small scar was one, he carried no battle scars. There were some burn scars on his forearms and one on his shoulder, evidence of his craft as a bladesmith. Perhaps his battle scars were on his legs?

"Here," he said, handing her several mostly dried leaves. He stuffed several in his mouth and chewed them.

She sniffed the leaves. Mint. *Ah. For my breath and my digestion.* She nodded her thanks and placed them in her mouth, resisting the irrational urge to breathe into her cupped hand and check her breath.

Silje looked away, down at the pot, her thoughts racing, chewing meditatively. Would her father be pleased with Liam? He had wanted to marry her to a man of his choosing. A farmer or a fisherman or a trader, aye, but these also knew how to fight when called upon. Liam seemed to prefer to talk instead. Yet—she glanced at the three *Skrælingjar* sitting across from

131

her, patiently waiting for the meal to be ready—yet in this instance she could hardly fault him.

"I almost forgot," Liam said, hurriedly putting on a clean under-tunic. He grinned at her and then at the warriors. "Merry Christmas!"

Christmas! By all that is holy, he's of the new faith! Silje smiled, though inwardly she cringed. Her father was not of the new faith. She sighed and reminded herself, again, that she didn't even want a husband. Oddly, she didn't seem as strongly opposed today. Had Liam cast some spell upon her?

The center warrior—the speaker—said something and Liam responded while he donned another tunic over the first. He squatted by the fire, took the spoon from her, and checked on the porridge all while continuing what seemed like a tale. He pulled the pot off the fire. The warriors put a hand inside their robes and came out with a leather sack each. They opened their bags and retrieved three large clam shells.

Liam scooped up the hot porridge with their shells, feeding their guests first. He dug in his pack and brought out a spoon for her. He scooped his large spoon full and then indicated that she should eat from the pot. He and the warriors ate the thick, sweetish oat mush without utensils, merely biting off portions directly from the shells or the large spoon. After the porridge was gone, the speaker offered the fish to them first, and then the three *Skrælingjar* partook. Liam passed around the water skin that he'd refilled at the stream.

It was time to break camp and return to her people. Silje tightened her jaw and stood.

"We should go as soon as you've packed," she said to Liam. He cocked his head at her and gave her a sympathetic smile. *Why sympathetic?*

"It is not the custom of our guests for the men to pack," Liam explained. "As my *wife* they will expect you to do that chore."

"Me?"

"Sorry."

"You take advantage of my good nature, *husband*," she

managed to grate out around her clenched teeth.

"It is a reasonable custom," he added, trying unsuccessfully to appear guileless. "If you apply your reasoning, you will find it so as well."

"Doubtful," she muttered.

"Men are the warriors. They protect their families from intruders and they hunt for food. To do that, they must have their hands free. They cannot be caught up in domestic chores. These *Skrælingjar* do not live behind barricades where they might relax their vigilance."

"And yet *I* am the warrior."

"We are keeping our guests comfortable. Is that not a Norse tradition?"

Silje glared at him. "Do you expect me to wash the pot and spoon as well?"

Liam sensibly kept his mouth shut and merely nodded.

He watched Silje march away to the stream, pot in one hand and spoon in the other. He kept an eye on her while he continued the tale of Christmas. Perhaps when the Jesuit priests come in the seventeenth century to convert the natives, this tale would be part of their mythology and so their conversion to Christianity might come more readily. The elder Mi'kmaq shared one of their legends with him while they waited patiently for Silje to return.

Liam recalled the feel of her beneath him last night and the sense of rightness he experienced when she slept in his arms. He decided that he wasn't going to give her up. He belonged to her and she belonged to him. It wasn't a modern notion but he didn't care. Somehow, he would make this declared bonding stand.

When Silje returned, she set the pot near the fire to dry.

"Thank you," Liam said, smiling up at her. "Give me your hands."

"Why?"

"They must be freezing," he murmured, capturing them and folding her icy hands within his warm palms. He brought them to his mouth and breathed hot air on them.

Her only response to his kindness was to compress her lips. He released her and she turned to their bed. She rolled up the bear-skin sleeping bag and bound it together with strips of rawhide that he handed her.

"Is helping permitted?" she muttered. "Will your new friends not object and think less of you if you give me any aide?"

"They will not think less of *me*," Liam replied calmly. "They will think less of *you* if you cannot do this simple task. I want them to respect you."

Silje's expression softened and she gave a single nod of thanks. She repacked his *neverkont*, tucking his dirty shirt around the dry pot.

Liam held up his comb and the three warriors immediately stood. They withdrew into the forest to give them privacy.

"Here, Silje," he said, resettling himself in a kneeling position. "Come and sit with me and I will comb your hair for you."

She scowled and faced him with her hands on her hips.

"Only a woman as beautiful as yourself could look so lovely with your hair in a tangle."

Silje touched her hands to her braids. Liam might be silver-tongued but he was also right. Running through the woods, hiding under a log in the dried leaves and then a night's repose had not left her hair in good order. No one had combed her hair for her since her mother died two years since. She succumbed to Liam's coaxing gaze. He took her hand and pulled her down to sit cross-legged in front of him, facing the fire. His powerful thighs encompassed her hips and she swallowed thickly at the sensation they brought. His fingers teased the metal hair binders from the ends of her braids. Shivers danced along her spine with each touch.

She cleared her throat and then asked, "Why did they move off? Have they gone?"

"Nay. When a husband combs his wife's hair, it's a private

thing."

"Oh." There they were again. Those two words. *Husband. Wife.*

Liam took exquisite care untangling her hair.

"How did you know that? How did you know they would leave us alone?"

"My grandmother was *Skræling.*"

Silje started and looked over her shoulder at him.

"Whoa, be careful." He caught the braid he'd been in the midst of making, tugged free by her sudden movement.

"You do not look like *Skræling.*"

Liam shrugged and gently turned her head around so she faced forward. "I suppose the blood of my grandfather's ancestors is strong in my veins. My father was a Norse trader."

"And your grandmother? She told you of their customs?"

"Aye."

"I see. She taught you their language?" She expected ready assent and so Liam's long pause confused her. Silje started to turn her head again but he held it in place and clicked his tongue at her. She pressed him for an answer. "She taught you their language?"

Liam sighed. "Nay, she did not. Only a word or two. Mostly curses, actually. Nan loved to curse. There are no proper curse words in the *Skræling* language, but she would cobble a few likely candidates together and depend on her tone of voice to convey her true meaning."

Silje smiled at his loving tone of voice. And yet, he had not told her how he could speak the native language.

"If she did not teach you, then how did you learn it?" Silje waited patiently while Liam finished her hair, holding out his hand for the metal clamps that would bind the braid ends. He rested his hands on her shoulders. "Speak. I will listen."

"It is a gift. When I hear another language, I can immediately understand it and speak it back."

Silje twisted around so she faced him. His expression showed earnest regard. He was not teasing her with a false answer. "What manner of gift is this? Who gave it to you?"

He took a deep breath and pressed his lips together. Then he raised his empty hands in a gesture of surrender.

"A strange old woman gave it to me. She kissed me on the lips and said, 'I've given you the gift of tongues, Liam. It will prove useful.'"

Silje answered him in the Frankish tongue. *"She was a witch, then?"*

"I'm not sure. Perhaps?" He took another deep breath, puffing out his cheeks before letting the air go in a whoosh of sound. He rubbed his eyebrow with a knuckle and added, *"I suppose she must have been because now we are speaking Frankish."*

"All good gifts come from God," Silje asserted, reverting to her native language.

Liam's insides unclenched. She believed him. If he told her all, would she believe he'd come from another time? He thrust that aside and closely examined her earnest expression.

"Silje? Are you...are you a Christian? Have you set the old gods aside and are now worshiping the one true God?"

"I am," she said, straightening her shoulders. "My mother and I converted when a priest came through our lands and taught us the true religion. It is King Olaf Tryggvason's desire that all convert. My father would not. He still worships Odin and Thor."

Liam grasped at this new information. King Olaf Tryggvason had ruled Norway for only five years—from 995 a.d. to 1000 a.d. This substantiated his guess so far. Now he knew *when* he lived, give or take a few years. It astonished him at how grounded he felt with this new knowledge.

"Silje, I'm confused. Leif Erikson discovered Vinland. Why are you here if your family is from Norway, not Greenland?"

"Because my father would not convert, he sailed with all who would follow him to Erik the Red's colony of Greenland." Silje scowled. "Jarl Erik will also not convert. He despises, aye, and distrusts the new religion. Things will change when his son, Leif, is our ruler for he and his wife have both abandoned the old religion. Leif's mother also converted and built us a church in which to worship."

Liam clasped his hands in his lap and rocked them back and forth as he thought. *I have to throw my lot in with Silje and her people. How else am I going to be able to leave here? I must stay with Silje.* The subject of his thoughts placed a hand over his rocking fists. He glanced up at her, catching her solemn expression.

"Tell me your thoughts," she ordered.

He cleared his throat first, then asked, "When we rejoin the rest of your party, will we be returning to Leif's settlement or will we be returning to your home in Greenland?"

"We?"

"You will not leave me here," Liam said, gesturing around him.

"Do you not wish to return to Eire? To your family there?"

Liam turned his hands over and clasped hers. "I have no family there. I am alone." He lifted her hands and kissed her knuckles. "Unless I am with you and then I won't be alone."

He held his breath, waiting for her response.

Chapter Seven

Silje withdrew her hands from his warm clasp. She smoothed her braids, following their length with her trembling fingers. This man, this man whom she met only yesterday—nay, last night—who had 'pretended' to be married to her in front of witnesses...now wanted to claim her and her family for his own. The remembrance of his lips on hers came to her in full force. Color heated her cheeks.

This is not like me, she thought, furious with herself. *I am not a young maiden to blush and fidget before a suitor. Maiden, aye, but not young. I have twenty and two years and I am not a fool!*

"Silje?" Liam took back her hands and stared into her eyes with his beautiful brown ones. "I know I am not a warrior, but I have other skills. And, my lovely shield-maiden, you can teach me how to fight."

"You don't have a sword," she pointed out, crinkling her eyes at him.

Liam threw back his head and laughed. He wiped the edges of his eyes and said, a grin in his voice, "I will have to make me another one, won't I?"

Silje returned a perfunctory smile, furious with herself for acting like a maiden meeting her betrothed for the first time.

Liam sobered. "What is it? Is there another you favor? Someone back home in Greenland perhaps?"

Silje almost laughed but then she'd have to explain her mirth and that would be unbearable. "Nay. 'Tis not that."

"Then what? Is it that we just met? Only..." he paused and glanced at his wrist. There was nothing there. He covered the ring of whiter skin, evidence of a wrist band long worn but no longer, with his other hand. "...Uh, only a dozen or so hours ago?"

Silje widened her eyes and gave a half-shrug. *So little*

time. And yet, it seemed as though they'd known each other longer.

"Something else?"

She gathered her courage and blurted, "Liam, I cannot cook." He frowned and she rushed on. "I never wanted to learn. I never wanted to marry. I have always wished to be a shield-maiden."

He considered her for several long heartbeats. She held her breath. *What is he thinking? Has his desire for me passed?*

"Silje. Do you wish to live in your father's longhouse until he dies?"

She shook her head. How she longed to be without her father's direct control, to be her own person, not just the chieftain's daughter. But, to replace her father with the will of a stranger? Was that what she wanted?

"And *I* can cook," Liam confessed in a secretive whisper. He bounced his eyebrows. "It's one of my skills."

Silje opened her mouth but no sound came out.

"Tell you what," he said, pulling her to her feet as he rose. "We've got a long walk back to your camp. Lots of time for you to think."

"You also."

"Not so much. I've already made my decision. You are what I want," he replied simply. Liam tilted her chin and pressed a lingering kiss onto her lips. Her fingertips brushed his cheek in a feather-like touch. He drew back and gave her a crooked smile. "I hate to say this, but our friends are going to expect you to carry my pack."

Silje instantly scowled. Liam chuckled softly and she swatted him on the arm. She recoiled, horrified at her familiarity but he only laughed out loud and hugged her. Hugged...her. No man hugged her. Not her father. Not her uncle or her cousins. Her younger brother used to but he'd been lost at sea on the journey from Norway to Greenland.

"In the *Skræling* tradition, the one who carries the weapons does not carry the pack. Women carry packs."

Silje patted the sword hilt. "I am wearing my sword and

carrying your shield. You have only an axe."

"Only an axe?" Liam asked, his surprise evident.

"A sword is superior to an axe."

After her proud boast he said something that puzzled her. "Next thing I know, we'll be playing rock, paper, scissors but it will be called sword, axe and shield."

"What was that?" Silje demanded.

"Oh, nothing. Nothing," he replied, laughing to himself. Liam plucked his cloak off one end of the lean-to. "Here. You can't be warm without a cloak. Wear mine."

"I will not," Silje shot back. She tugged her fur-lined jerkin into place. "I have this to keep me warm. I am not cold."

Liam watched her from beneath a beetling brow. Was this the moment when he imposed his will on her? Again? *I should have punched him, not just slapped his arm.* Then his expression lightened.

"I have just the thing." He swung his cloak around him, attached it with a brooch and moved to his *neverkont*—one of the largest packs she'd ever seen.

Liam rummaged around until he found the woolen hand-woven brown and white striped scarf from the Christmas cracker. He brought it out, shook it, folded it diagonally, and wrapped it around Silje's neck, tucking it gently into the top of her tunic, lifting her braids out of the way.

"This should help keep you warm," he said, stroking the line of her jaw with one finger before holding her away from him so he could see it on her. "Very nice."

Silje fingered the soft fabric. "Who wove this for you? Did you buy it at a market in Eire?"

"Nay. The old Aunty gave it to me."

She blinked and her hand stilled. "The same who gave you the gift of tongues?"

"Aye, the same."

In a low whisper, she asked, "Is it magic then?"

"Now there's a good question. I don't know. Honest." He pursed his lips and wiggled them from side to side once as he thought. "I wouldn't bet on it." Liam glanced around. "Did you see my helm? I almost forgot about it."

"There, at the base of that tree." She pointed to where his belt hung. He headed toward it. "A true warrior does not forget his equipment."

Liam looked over his shoulder at her. "Lesson number one? Very well. A warrior remembers his equipment." He strapped his belt on over his cloak and picked up his helm. Liam recalled that he'd leant his folding shovel next to the helm. It was gone. He suspected his sketchpad and pencil had disappeared too. He brought the helm back to his pack and retrieved the cap he needed to wear under it, checking around for the sketchpad and pencil he'd kept in an inside pouch. *Damn. Too bad.* He found his flint, though, and was glad of it.

Liam straightened, donned the cap and deliberately put the helm on wrong to see if Silje would comment.

She clicked her tongue and came closer. "It's on backward," she said, holding up her hands. He leaned over so she could adjust it and buckle the strap under his chin once the helm was on right. She stood back and surveyed him. "There's not a dent in your helm. That's very telling. Take it off."

"Why?" he asked, reaching for the buckle.

"Give it to me," she ordered, holding out an impatient hand. He passed it over and then watched, amazed, when she banged it against a rock a couple of times, leaving a few dents in the pristine curves. She looked it over before she rubbed it into the forest floor debris, and finally against the moss on the side of a tree. "There. That's improved."

Liam blinked rapidly and took the helm back. He drew in a deep breath and gave a short laugh. "You're trying to hide that I'm not a warrior, aren't you?"

Silje nodded. "You are a big man—as big as my father and my uncle. They will expect you to know how to fight."

"I have taken lessons," Liam said, grimacing at the inadequacies of 21st century sparring. "Yet I have never been in a battle nor have needed to swing an axe or a sword against another in anger."

"From what manner of world have you come, Liam O'Brien? I have not heard that Eire is so full of peace that a man stays innocent of battle experiences."

Liam shrugged. "I am no coward. The need to fight, however, has never come my way."

Silje snorted and then grinned. "It will now. I will teach you what I know."

"Have you been to battle?" Liam asked, closing his pack and tying the sleeping bag on top of it.

Silje shook her head, her lips pressed tightly together. "My father would not give me a sword and would not let me come into battle with him when I only had a bow and arrow to support him. I have fought off bandits before, though, with only my knife and a small axe used for kindling."

"Oh, that's bad," Liam murmured, heaving the pack up onto his back. He kept his reflections to himself. It wasn't his place to be glad that she'd never been directly involved in the bloody business of war.

Silje clucked her tongue and tugged his cloak into place beneath the pack.

"My thanks."

"Since my brother died, my father's one desire is for me to marry so I might give him grandsons," she said, her voice heavy with scorn. "If he wanted so many males, he should have covered my mother more often."

Liam looked at her in surprise.

She sighed. "My apologies. The memory of my mother deserves more respect." She shifted her weight from one side to another. "She's been dead these past two years."

Liam touched her on the shoulder. "I'm sorry. My mother has also passed on." She nodded once. He looked beyond her. "Ah, here are our guests."

Silje swung around, her hand tightening on the pommel of her sword.

"Easy," he murmured. To the Mi'kmaq he said, "We're ready to go."

The elder native warrior said, "You let your woman

defend you?"

Liam smiled. "Her skill surpasses my own." He patted his axe. "Besides, I can still get to my own weapon. Let's go."

They followed the three *Skrælingjar*. Silje carefully observed their surroundings for landmarks. She did not trust the native men to lead them back to her camp and not off to their village, unwilling sacrifices in a pagan ceremony. She couldn't help but think, *like goats to the slaughter*. Her mad flight through the woods had not caused her to lose her excellent sense of direction.

"I bet we run into searchers before we reach your camp, luv," Liam said, pausing to hold a branch out of the way for her.

"Aye. We were scheduled to leave on the afternoon tide today," Silje said, passing beneath his arm so that he took up the rear. She chose to ignore his endearment and in particular, she chose to ignore her pleasure in it. Love in Norse marriages usually came after their marriage, if it came at all. Since she had never planned on marrying, she'd never concerned herself with that elusive emotion.

"How many ships do you have?"

"Two *knerrir*. The merchant vessels provide us with safer passage through the open seas than longships. They also require fewer men to handle them. Our group is thirty men strong. We have two female Sami thralls who cook and wash for us."

"You are the only shield-maiden?"

"Aye. I am that. My father's brother is our leader on this expedition. He did not want me to come but I came anyway. I wanted to explore, not sit idle, tending kitchen fires and arguing with my father, who is chieftain."

"A Jarl?"

"Nay, merely the chief amongst those of us who followed him from our home in Norway."

They climbed over two mushroom-covered logs and down through a gully and back up again before Liam asked another question.

"What manner of man is your father? From what you have said already, he sounds a hard man. Is my understanding correct?"

"Oh, aye. He is that. But he is clever too." She stopped and turned around to face him. She jabbed a finger into his chest. "Do not underestimate him, Liam O'Brien."

He clasped her hand and smiled down at her. "I won't, luv. Thank you for the warning."

Silje tugged her hand free and returned to following the *Skrælingjar*. *Why does my heart betray me when Liam smiles? My stomach, too, feels as if it is made from clouds. The winds of my emotions blow it about as if it...as if I could float! I do not want this sensation and yet I find I like it. What is amiss with me?*

They hiked for three hours and did not come across a road, paved or otherwise. They crossed two paths but neither were double tracks, indicating the use of carts or tractors or anything smacking of technology. Whenever they entered open clearings, Liam searched the blue skies for jet trails. It was a vain hope but he searched for them anyway for if he saw even one, he would know he was the victim of an elaborate practical joke. He saw none. The conviction that he'd been transported back in time settled deeper and deeper into his bones. He rolled his shoulders and accepted the truth he'd sensed during the night.

Liam stayed quiet for a time, briefly mourning the friends he'd left behind—Charlie in particular. When his friend returned to pick him up in two weeks, what would he do? He'd park his truck and start searching for him. *And I won't be there. Even my shelter and fire circle followed me here. Will he find my watch and shovel? A pile of foil food packs? My sketch pad and pencil? If he does, then he'll think something happened to me. And he'll be right, I guess. There'll be a search and rescue party called out. How long will they search for me? When will Charlie give up? Never,* he thought, his

144

heart heavy. *He'll go the rest of his life wondering what happened to me.*

"You are quiet," Silje said, grabbing his hand as he lifted her out of a dip and over a log. "My thanks."

Liam nodded in return. He gave her a little smile and left it at that. How could he explain his sadness to her? Explanations such as that required privacy and time.

Time.

He took a deep breath and set Charlie's future to the side. There was nothing he could do about his friend's life any more. He had his own to worry about.

"Liam?"

He glanced down. "Aye?"

Silje was not looking at him. She nodded beyond the Mi'kmaq warriors ahead of them. "I believe we have more guests."

Liam turned and looked, saying, "Your family? Or more *Skrælingjar?*"

"That's my uncle. And two of my cousins. They do not look pleased."

Liam snorted and grabbed her by the elbow, hurrying her along. "You describe their expressions too mildly, luv. *I* think they look bloody furious."

Chapter Eight

Three Viking warriors emerged from a break in the forest some fifty paces ahead and slightly above them. They wore their helms and carried drawn swords and shields, looking fierce and powerful. One was older and clearly the father of the other two men. Their identical straight noses betrayed their kinship. A scar bisected the father's left cheek, running from the corner of his eye down to his jaw. All three had strawberry-blond hair, woven into thick braids. Gray streaked Silje's uncle's beard. Their cloaks flapped in the breeze.

They could've stepped right out of a painting, Liam thought in an off-handed way.

One son, taller than the other, lifted his sword arm in salute. His expression remained calm and thoughtful. His brother, however, scowled mightily and banged his sword against his yellow and white painted shield.

"The one making so much noise is Fritjof. His disposition suits his name for Fritjof means 'one who steals peace'," Silje explained, hastening forward with Liam at her side. "The other is Audun. He is slow to anger and is thoughtful."

"And your uncle?" Liam asked, keeping his voice low. "What is his name?"

"Ivar Sigurdson. He is a fierce fighter but a sensible leader."

The three Mi'kmaq warriors paused, still in the open. They stood to one side so Liam and Silje could draw even with them.

"These are your people?" the leader asked.

"Yes. The elder man is my wife's uncle."

"Are they searching for your wife?" the speaker asked, a tinge of suspicion in his voice.

"They have come to meet us, merely." Liam hoped he exuded confidence. "They are anxious to leave this place and sail across the sea to their home. See? Her cousin is annoyed that we did not arrive sooner. I'm certain he worries that we will miss the tide and will not be able to leave until tomorrow."

The eldest Mi'kmaq warrior grunted.

"Silje Petursdotter! Where have you been?" Ivar demanded, taking several steps toward them. "And who is this?" he asked, pointing his sword at Liam. "From whence has he come?"

Liam held his breath, waiting for Silje's answer. She scowled.

"This is Liam O'Brien," she stated. After a long pause, she added, "My husband."

The affect on the three men varied. Her uncle frowned. Her cousin Audun smiled. Her other cousin Fritjof took a hasty step forward.

"Nay," he gasped. "'Tis not so. You lie."

"Call me a liar again, Fritjof and I'll cut the tongue from your mouth," Silje shot back.

"You were to marry me!" her cousin shouted. "Me! Not some stranger who has taken you without your father's permission."

Silje snarled in return. "I am not a child who cannot make her own choices. Nor am I a piece of furniture to be given to a man of my father's choosing."

Liam held up his empty hands. "Peace. Peace. We are confusing our *Skræling* guests. They believe they are escorting a newly married couple back into the arms of their relatives. We must take care." The three Viking warriors narrowed their gazes at him. "Please try to look like you're happy to see us." To the Mi'kmaq, he said, a rueful smile twisting his lips, "As you can hear, they are not pleased we failed to hurry back."

Ivar spoke. "You speak their tongue?"

"Aye, he can," Silje stated proudly. "He speaks many tongues."

Audun entered into the conversation for the first time. He had a strong, measured way of speaking. "We are not far from our camp. We had sentries watching for your return and we came as soon as they sent word of you. There is a tale here to be told and I would like to hear it next to a fire with a bowl of stew warming my hands."

"An excellent notion," Liam replied, nodding at the taller cousin. Once more turning to the Mi'kmaq, Liam said, "Our fire is waiting. Will you share its warmth with us?"

The speaker shook his head. "Our own fires await our return. But, hear this, tall warrior. We will come again in three days and we will bring many warriors with us. It would be best if we could not find your camp."

"*Ever*," the eldest Mi'kmaq warrior added. "We have long memories."

"I understand," Liam said, bowing his shoulders to them. "My wife and I thank you for your company."

The Mi'kmaq warriors turned and faded into the woods.

"Where have they gone?" Ivar demanded, marching right up to them. His two sons followed directly behind him. When he stopped, they ranged on either side of their father.

"Home, I expect," Liam said. He held out his arm. "I am Liam O'Brien of Eire."

Ivar hesitated and then clasped him about the forearm and then released him. Liam offered his hand to Audun, who took it. Fritjof ignored his gesture. Liam stepped back and hooked his thumbs through his belt. *Perpetuate the lie.* "Several days back, *Skrælingjar* attacked my shipmates while I was separated from them and they had to put to sea without me. I suspect they think I'm dead."

"How long have you known this…this…" Fritjof stumbled into a huff.

"Long enough, cousin," Silje said, glaring at him.

Ivar sheathed his sword and nodded to his sons to do likewise. He faced his niece. "Declarations were made before witnesses?" he demanded, narrowing his gaze.

Silje knew this was the last moment when she might back out of this marriage. All she had to do was allow them to believe the declaration had been forced.

"Silje?" Ivar prompted. "What say you?"

She glanced at Liam and wished he'd smile. A little smile was all she needed to reassure her that this path was the right one. Even a twitch of his lips would prove sufficient.

He grinned. A wide, open smile that showed his perfect white teeth. And then he winked at her. Silje's stomach transformed into an airy cloud once more.

"Aye," she said, smiling back. "Declarations were made before witnesses."

"Before the *Skrælingjar*?" Fritjof scoffed.

Silje lost her smile. "You cannot undo our joining by denying the validity of our witnesses." She took half a step toward him. "I would never have married you, cousin, for your temper is uncertain and you have not yet finished growing up!"

"I have two years on you and four battles to my name," he protested with considerable heat.

"That is not enough," she replied, turning away from him. "Uncle?"

Her uncle was not looking at her. He was looking at the sword on her belt. He pointed at it.

"Was this your husband's morning-gift?"

"Aye," she said, drawing the shining blade.

Even Fritjof's sputtering wrath disappeared at the sight of the beautifully made sword. Her uncle reached for it and she reluctantly let him take Gut Slasher. He tested its weight and looked along its length, checking for a warp. He shaved the hair off the back of one hand with the sword edge. He shook his head and wonder shone from his eyes. Both his sons leaned around him to catch a look at the blade.

"Your father—"

"My father cannot refuse me my morning-gift." Silje held out her hand. With obvious reluctance, Ivar returned it to her. Silje sheathed it. "Gut Slasher is mine. I have a sword at long last."

"You bound yourself to a stranger for a sword?" Fritjof asked in a whisper. "A sword?"

"For such a sword men have killed their own brothers,"

Silje said.

Liam cleared his throat and they all looked at him. He raised his eyebrows.

"I do not wish to break up this reunion, but I think I should mention that our friends," he nodded toward where the three *Skrælingjar* disappeared, "have given us a warning that we have three days to set sail or they will be annoyed."

"They will have no chance against the might of our sword arms," Fritjof declared, resting his hand on the hilt of his sword.

"I have no doubt," Liam said, glancing his way and then at Silje's uncle. "And yet we will incur more ill will amongst those who live in these lands if we do not heed their warning. When Leif Erikson wishes to return and collect more furs and more trees and more food, it would be best if he was not met with open hostility. There is also the risk to your cargo. If your ships are burned, all will be lost. It is a long, long, *long* walk back home."

"Aye," Ivar said, nodding sharply. "Silje's husband speaks true." He turned around, slapped his youngest son on the shoulder, and started up the incline. "Come. Tomorrow's outgoing tide will be soon enough. We cannot leave on today's as we are not ready. We could not leave without you, girl, so our preparations were delayed while we searched for you. There are three teams still to return."

"I am pleased you searched for me," Silje muttered.

"Don't talk back, girl. You know I have the hearing of a hawk." He barked a laugh. "What caused you to run off? When you did not join us for the afternoon meal, we sent someone to fetch you. He found your basket of nuts and your discarded cloak. Aye, and your bow and quiver and bag of squirrels. There'll be squirrel stew tonight."

"I was set upon and ran."

Audun looked over his shoulder. "By the three *Skrælingjar* we met only moments since?"

Silje opened her mouth to respond to his question with the truth, caught Liam's look and altered her tale. "Nay. I lost the two who attacked me in the woods. If I'd had a *sword* I would have gutted them instead of hiding beneath a log like a cowering mouse." Her rancor caused her relatives to laugh. They'd heard such complaints before.

Ivar laughed loudest of all. When his mirth subsided, he said, "We shall feast tonight in celebration of your marriage, girl."

Silje pressed her lips together and then said, "Uncle, I am a girl no longer. The morning-gift has been paid."

He laughed again and she found herself blushing. Liam rested his hand on her shoulder. She glanced up at him and he smiled his approval and understanding.

"Aye, the morning-gift is given, but I have not seen the bride-price. You may not know this, Silje, but your father has set your value at twenty-four ounces of silver plus—"

Silje interrupted. "Twenty-four?" How could Liam pay her father a bride price of half that amount?

"Plus four goats," her uncle added.

Liam met Silje's shocked gaze. He squeezed her shoulder and then addressed her Uncle.

"Good Ivar, in the absence of Silje's father, are you to act as negotiator?"

"Aye, it would fall to me."

They paused as a group to look down at the beach where two merchant ships, fully loaded in anticipation of their departure, lay at anchor at the narrow end of Chaleur Bay, just past the estuary of the Restigouche River. About a dozen classic Viking tents dotted the shore above the high tide line. A shout went out below when those around several fires noted their arrival. Ivar raised his hand in acknowledgement.

"I would ask for a few moments to confer with my wife before we enter into negotiations."

Ivar's silvery-gray eyes considered him and then he cocked his head at his niece. "Be certain you want a man who cannot make his own decisions, gi— Silje."

Silje stiffened and glowered. "There is wisdom in a man

not being so foolish as to negotiate with a stranger when he can first take counsel with someone who knows his foe."

Ivar's eyebrows shot up and he scratched his golden-red and gray beard. "Sharp-tongued. That's what you are."

"And needle-witted," she claimed, raising her chin.

Her uncle chuckled and waved them over to a flat rock large enough to crouch upon. "When you are done conferring, come to my fire and eat your fill before the negotiations begin."

"Thank you," Liam replied. "We will not be long."

Ivar grunted and stalked off. Audun nodded genially to them and when Fritjof meant to linger, he grabbed his brother's arm and towed him away.

Liam walked with Silje over to the rock warmed by the mid-day sun. He swung his pack off his back and opened it.

"I did not see any silver amongst your belongings when I assembled them in your pack," Silje said. She tugged on one of her braids. "What shall we use for a bride-price?"

Liam set his *neverkont* on its side and crouched beside it. "Please, sit."

Silje glanced away at her fellow Norsemen and then positioned her body so she blocked their line of site. She crouched beside him. Liam removed his gloves and placed a warm palm against her cool cheek before kissing her hard on the lips.

He placed his forehead against hers and they both breathed heavily. "I will not give you up, my Silje," he swore and then drew back to look at her expression. She nodded once and stared at him, trust in her gaze. "Now, is there any chance your father will repudiate our marriage?"

Silje assured him. "Not once my uncle agrees to the bride-price."

"Then we'll have to get him to agree," Liam said. He shoved his long arm into the woven birch pack, all the way to the bottom where he'd tucked his bag of coins from the Christmas cracker. He grabbed hold of it and brought it out into the light. Liam bounced it a few times. "This might be enough."

"Is it silver?" she asked, whipping off her scarf and laying it on the stone.

Liam tipped it out. Coins tumbled out into a pile on the scarf. Silje hastily cupped her hands around them so none could escape.

"Oh, gold," she sighed. Her hand hovered over the pile of shiny coins. "How many?"

"I'm not certain. Let's count," he said, scooping them to one side and beginning to count. "Two, four, six, eight...thirty-eight, forty, forty-one. Forty-one. Is that enough?" he asked, meeting her beautiful blue eyes. The wonder in them turned to anger.

"You will *not* pay forty-one gold coins for me. That is well over the bride-price set by my father."

Liam shuffled closer. "There is the matter of the goats, remember."

Silje picked up a single coin. "Half of this one piece will buy six goats. He only wants four." She set this one to the side. She divided the pile. "This portion, here, is the equivalent of the twenty-four ounces of silver. We should not pay any more."

"That is less than half," Liam observed. "Will it be sufficient? I am willing to pay more."

"*I* am not. Think, husband. When we return to Greenland, we will have a forge to build and an adjacent house. My father has promised land as part of my dowry. We can build on that. There are furnishings and a thrall that were part of my mother's dowry that will come to us as well. But first we must have a place to live and work."

"Yes," Liam said, then his mind caught up with what he'd just heard. "Did you say thrall?"

"Aye. Kirste was my mother's thrall from before I was born."

"Silje, I cannot, nay, *we* cannot own a person," Liam said, a sour taste flooding his mouth at the mere thought of owning a slave.

"What will become of her if we do not take her?" Silje asked, tilting her head to one side. "My father uses her as one of his concubines. She does not care for him. And, husband, she is an excellent cook."

Liam passed a hand over his brow.

Silje touched his knee. "I can see this distresses you."

Liam took a deep breath before responding. "Silje, she must come to us, of course, if only to liberate her from your father's attentions, but, we must free her."

"Free her?" Silje sat back on her heels and thought. Her expression drifted away. "Aye. I think she would like that. I will miss her."

"We will hire her as a house servant," Liam promised. "If it is her wish."

Silje's attention returned to him and the gold. "We will need all the coin we can keep, Liam, else how will we pay Kirste? And you must buy tools for your trade."

"And coal for the forge. And...yes, I see your point." He gestured to the gold and to his pack and to his person. "Silje, I would have you know that you are worth *all* that I have. Even to the clothes on my back."

She flushed and looked pleased. Next, she said, a cunning expression coming over her face. "I thank you, husband, for your kind complement, but we must not let my uncle know you feel thus."

"Nay, you're right," Liam said, stroking his eyebrow.

Silje removed a handful of coins from one pile and set them in another. She pointed to the remaining ten coins. "This is sufficient. You will say that I am cantankerous—no one will disagree on this point. And defiant. And I am old."

Liam chuckled, then held up his hand when she glared at him. "Nay, do not be angry. How old are you?"

"I have twenty and two years, Liam. Old."

He shook his head and smiled warmly at her. "I have twenty and nine years. Am I old as well?"

"'Tis different. You are a man," she stated. He laughed again. "You must stop that. No one will believe you are unhappy with your choice if you laugh so much and look at me that way."

Liam sobered until only his lips twitched. "My apologies. I'll try to do better."

"Humph," she muttered, looking at him narrowly. "I am also bossy and I cannot cook."

"You always bring up your cooking as though this lack of skill is a great sin."

"I cannot sew either," she stated. "Or mend. Or grow food. We are unequally yoked, husband, for you bring many skills and I bring few."

Liam observed the line of pale skin around her mouth and realized these limitations affected her dearly even though she claimed her only desire was to be a shield-maiden.

"You have been busy learning other things," he said softly. Her jaw relaxed and she nodded. "If it means so much to you, Kriste can teach you to cook. My stomach growls and we have a strategy. Let us attend your uncle's fire and eat."

"And then negotiate my bride-price," Silje said, looking suddenly pale.

Liam scooped the money into the sack and put it back in the *neverkont*. "As little as possible, aye?"

"Aye. As little as possible."

Chapter Nine

Her father's men stepped respectfully aside when they walked through the group of tents to her own. They nodded at her and stared at Liam. Some folded their arms and stood with legs apart. Others rested their hands on their weapons. She introduced him as her husband to several of them when they passed. That caused a stir.

"This is our tent," Silje said, waving her hand at it.

"I like this," Liam murmured, reaching up and stroking the dragon-head carvings on the gable boards. "The work is very fine."

"Let's put your *neverkont* inside before we attend my uncle at his fire."

"Agreed," Liam said. He held back the flap for her to enter first. "Don't trip," he murmured, smiling at her. "Shall I carry you across the base board?"

"Unnecessary," she scoffed, carefully stepping over the threshold. For a bride to trip and fall would have been a bad omen for their marriage.

Liam entered behind her, a soft chuckle on his lips. He set his pack to one side, detached the sleeping bag and threw it down onto the top of her pallet. *Was he staking a claim?* Silje glanced at him but he was looking around the tent.

"Is it larger than the others?" he asked, stretching his arms out to the side and then overhead to the ridgepole. "It's great that we can stand up inside."

"You're smiling again."

"I'm happy," he replied, unrepentant, his hands now resting on his hips. "I smile when I'm happy."

"Heed my warning and act more sober," Silje said, raising her eyebrows. "My uncle will strip you of all your money if he thinks you are happy."

"I promise to act miserable," he swore and then kissed her.

"I'll just grab something from the pack and we'll go. I'm starving."

* * *

Silje paced inside her tent away from the prying eyes of the men, her hands on her hips and her head down. Her uncle had banished her before the bride-price negotiations began. Liam hadn't lived up to the promise to act miserable, but he had managed to act serious during the meal. *How much of his money will Uncle take from him? I should be there!*

Silje shivered and grabbed her cloak off the hook hanging from the ridgepole. She swung it around her shoulders and rubbed her arms for warmth. To distract herself from her annoyance at being left out she unrolled the sleeping bag and arranged it alongside her own and then unpacked Liam's things.

"Take care of your heart," she muttered, feeling the heat in her flushed cheeks at the sight of the two bags side-by-side. Again she recalled the feel and strength of him next to her. *There will be a true coupling here tonight. I must accustom myself to the idea. It is the way of things.*

Silje continued to think about how strange the event would be while she made piles of Liam's belongings so she could know the full extent of them. She reasoned out how the lamp worked, unfolded it, put the candle in place, and hung it from the hook suspended from the ridgepole above her head.

Perhaps I can convince my husband to wait until we know each other before we...do not be a fool, she admonished herself. *There will be no privacy in the longhouses. No privacy until we have built our own house. Do I expect him to wait until then? Months from now? At least in our own tent we can perform the first act without prying eyes.*

Silje sighed and shook her head, turning her scattered thoughts to the task at hand. She examined his clothing.

"These have not been worn," she mused, sitting back on her haunches, holding a finely made wool tunic on her lap. She peered more closely at the rest of the clothing—a difficult thing to do as the light was waning. All the clothes appeared

157

new. Even the dirty one. "How is that possible?"

A shadow filled the tent entrance and she glanced up.

"How is what possible?" Liam asked, stepping over the wooden threshold brace and into their tent.

She frowned at him. "Come out of the doorway, pray, so I might look at you."

Liam touched a thumb to the corner of his mouth and did as she asked. He looked at his thumb, licked it, and then grimaced at her.

"What has occurred?" she demanded, keeping her voice down. She pointed to a low stool.

Liam grabbed hold of it and sat next to her. She rose to her knees and grasped his chin, turning it this way and that. She scowled. "You've been fighting and you smell like mead."

Her husband captured her hand and kissed it. She snatched her hand away and folded her arms, sitting back on her heels.

"Nay, fighting is too strong a word for it," he said, lifting one corner of his mouth in a crooked smile. After a minatory stare, he continued, "Your cousin Fritjof took exception to our marriage. I guess he doesn't think me a fit person to be your husband. We had words. He hit me and I knocked him down. He fell pretty hard, actually. Then your other cousin, Audun, shoved a jug of mead in my hand and we all shared a swig or two. Or five or six in the case of Fritjof, truth be told. I don't think he'll be giving us any more trouble."

"Men," Silje said pithily.

Liam grinned and shrugged. "Now, what was that you were muttering to yourself when I came in? What's not possible?"

Silje allowed herself to be distracted. She held up one of his tunics. In a whisper, she said, "All of your clothes are new. Did you wear the same set of clothing crossing the ocean and then discard them upon your arrival in Vinland? There are no soiled clothes here except for the one tunic."

Liam shook his head. He handed her his leather purse. She took it and hefted the bag and then scowled up at him.

"What is this? How much did my uncle ask for the bride-price? This feels much as it did when you took it earlier. You must have struck a goodly bargain."

Liam moved off the stool and crouched beside her, took the tunic away, folded it and put it back in the pile before he answered.

"I bargained hard. You would have been proud of me," he said, grinning at her. "I swear I did not smile or laugh. Your uncle discussed all your good points. Your beauty. Your position in the clan. He praised your strength of purpose in becoming a Christian. He extolled your virtue and your physical prowess."

"He has a lying tongue," she muttered, secretly pleased.

Liam laughed and stroked a hand down the back of her head. Her heartbeat tripped.

"What did you say? Oh, how I wished I'd been there."

"I agreed with everything he said."

"What folly!" she exclaimed softly. Silje bit her lip to keep from smiling. "Did you not complain about my obstinacy? Did you not moan that I could not cook or do any of the other common tasks allotted to women?"

"Nay."

"But—"

"But I did mention your age," Liam admitted hurriedly, forestalling her scold.

Silje's heart clenched. "Oh…that is well. That must have brought my bride-price down."

"It did. I was amazed because I don't find you too old. Even so, I kept *all* our money."

Our money.

She narrowed her eyes. "What is this? How? My uncle knows my father would expect him to get the highest price for me. If my father wanted twenty-four ounces of silver, he would insist on not an ounce less. How did you pay the bride-price?"

"Uh," he stalled, rubbing his eyebrow with one knuckle. She glared and he confessed. "It occurred to me that I had something of more value than gold."

"What?"

"Cinnamon."

Silje's jaw dropped and she looked from him to his belongings, urgently searching for the bag she'd seen earlier that morning. She'd had a niggling feeling that something was missing. The bag held a small fist-sized amount of the precious spice. The bag was gone.

"Liam," she gasped, placing her hand on his arm. "In Greenland the spice is worth more than *all* our gold. Why did you pay so much? We agreed that you would pay as little as possible."

Liam covered her hand with his. "I wanted your family to know how highly I regard you. I told you before that you are worth all that I have."

Silje blinked at a sudden, unexpected tear. She bowed her head and turned away so he wouldn't see her weakness. Her husband rose and left. Silje brushed the tear away before he returned with a burning twig a moment later. He lit the lamp and then closed the flaps and tied them shut, sealing out the twilight and the interested men sitting around the campfires.

"There, that should give us some privacy," he said softly. "Are you warm enough? Mist is coming in off the bay."

"Aye," she said, swallowing hard after the single syllable. "Let's repack my stuff."

"Are you angry that I pried into your belongings?"

"Nay. Why? You are my wife. What's mine, is yours. Did you find anything else interesting?"

Plucking at the reprieve, Silje picked up the blue leather tube. She laid it across her palm and held it out. "This. What is in this? It feels empty, yet when I shake it, something rattles inside."

"Didn't you look?" her husband asked.

She shook her head. He seemed tense. *Is it because of the coupling ahead? Why should he be tense? He's the one who has done it before.*

"Just a moment and I'll tell you."

He quickly repacked his things and then sat down on the bear-fur beside her. Silje's first instinct was to put more distance between them but then her natural desires took over. She wanted to sit close to him and feel his warmth on her side. Silje hesitated and then leaned her head against his shoulder. Liam pressed his palm against her cheek for a brief time. *He cares for me. He must. His gestures. His expressions.* She recalled how he had warmed her hands with his own breath this morning. *His kindnesses. His respect.*

"Now, this is a fantastic tale," Liam warned, taking his hand from her cheek and retrieving the blue tube from her hand. "And you may not believe it, but I promise you it is true."

Silje sat up straight and twisted around so she could look him in the face. By the golden glow of the candle, she watched the expression on his face as he spoke in a voice so low she had to strain to hear it.

"Three days ago my friend, Charlie, and I attended a fair near-by as planned."

"Here?" Silje asked just as quietly, pointing at the ground. "In this part of Vinland?"

"Aye."

"How is that possible? Is there another Norse settlement here?"

Liam shook his head. "Nay. At least, none that I know of."

"But you said your shipmates left you behind."

"Aye, that's what I said." Liam stared her in the eye. "I lied."

Silje scowled. *He lied!* She started to stand but paused at his next words, spoken in a quietly commanding voice.

"You will let me finish, please."

Liam held his breath, praying that Silje would relax and listen to him. She pressed her lips into a thin line, gave a single nod, and settled back down. *Have I blown it?* Liam let out his breath and decided he'd best get on with it now that he'd started. He didn't want to make love to her with this massive secret between them. Surely he would need to lie again in the future to establish his false history, but he wanted her in on the lies, not a victim of them.

"I had to lie because the truth is impossible to believe."

"Speak on."

Liam examined her expression and couldn't tell anything more than that she was angry. Her breath came in uneven, small puffs as though she held her breath between exhalations. Liam unfolded his legs and placed one alongside her hip, feeling that physical contact between them would help her accept his story. Her eyes widened at the contact. Thankfully, she didn't move away. Hope flared.

I've got to trust her. We cannot move forward with this lie between us. If she repudiates me—he shuddered—*then I will have to make my home with the Mi'kmaq and lose her forever.*

"It was at the fair that I met the old Aunty," he said, clenching his gut and listening closely to his bones. He waved his hand at the *neverkont*. "That's where I bought most of my gear. The sleeping bag, the clothes, even my boots and sandals."

"But—"

Liam held up his hand and she scowled again.

"I promise, I'll tell you everything." He waited for her to object but she waived him onward. "And she gave me this," he said, holding up the tube. "As a Christmas gift."

"As well as the gift of tongues?" she asked. "Was that a true tale or a falsehood?"

"Nay. That was true. After she gave me this, she kissed me on the lips and bestowed on me the gift of tongues. I didn't realize what she meant at first. At our noon meal, Charlie asked me something in the Germanic tongue and I understood him completely and I could talk back to him as well."

Some of the wonder he'd felt must have shown in his face and in his voice for her expression softened a little. Heartened, he continued his tale.

"Yesterday morning, I left my lodgings with all my new gear. Charlie traveled with me for some of the distance and then we went our separate ways. I hiked into the woods and set up my camp—the camp where you found me." He opened the blue-leather tube and took out the remnants of the Christmas cracker. Liam placed both pieces in her hands. She examined everything carefully and then returned them to him. "This used to be closed," he said, indicating the separate ruffle. "Incredibly, in spite of its small size, the inside was full of other gifts from the old Aunty. Your scarf, my handkerchief, my brooch, a slip of paper with a proverb on it, the bag of money, my flute, and a sweet. I ate the sweet," he said with a shrug and a half smile. She didn't smile back and he grimaced. After taking a deep breath, he said, "I opened it at the appointed hour just as instructed. Everything changed after that."

"What changed?" Silje asked softly as he paused in reverie. Her hand wrapped around his leg and she leaned toward him. "Tell me all."

"I did not realize the change at first. I went to sleep thinking all was the same. And then you arrived and I met you and the *Skrælingjar*. None of you belonged. My watch was gone and the rusty iron boss I'd discovered just that day was transformed into a proper shield. My bones were itching. Things weren't *right*."

Silje broke in on his near rant. "Husband. I do not take your meaning."

In an anguished shush, Liam spit out the truth. "Silje. I am not from this time."

"What say you?" she demanded, straightening. Her nostrils flared and she tightened her grip on his leg.

"I am from a time far in your future," he revealed in a bare whisper, ever aware that a canvas tent wall blocked no sound. He leaned toward her and she didn't draw back. "I did not believe it myself when the understanding first came to me. I came from over one thousand years in the future. I studied the Norse culture. I searched for artifacts from this time. That was my trade. My things look new because they *are* new." He shook his head in wonder. "They are new. The clothes, my pack, everything."

Will she believe me? Can she believe me? In this time of

mythology and legends and magic? Christianity is a new religion for the Norse and surely it has not wiped away all the superstitions of the converted? She believes me about the gift of tongues. Will she believe me in this...this enormous truth?

Silje swallowed and licked her lips. She tilted her head and then breathed out her next words. "The old witch. Aunty. She is responsible?"

"Aye. It had to be her."

Silje stared into his eyes. Her own were troubled. Her jaw worked and her hand opened and closed spasmodically on the leg he'd pressed against her hip. "Liam, from all that you've told me since I first found you in the woods, what is true? Did you make my sword?"

"Aye. And my knife, and the axe, and the spoon. The shield appeared out of nowhere, as I've said. Aunty must be responsible for that as well."

"And your name? Is your name true?"

"Aye. I am Liam O'Brien and my grandmother was *Skræling*, though we do not call them that in my time. They're called Mi'kmaq. The story about the goats was true, too. And I *can* cook." He leaned forward and in an urgent undertone, he whispered, "Silje. *My* Silje. I am the same man you laid beside last night. My origin should not matter. I promise you I have the skills to make a good husband. I can hunt with a bow. I can forge and build. I am slow to anger and quick to forgive. Forgive me now, please, for the lies I told."

Silje stared at him, her thoughts racing. Whenever his origins, she could not lose this man. Could her longing for him be any less fantastic than the tale he told? Could her desire for a *husband* be any less mystical than his journey through time? She had never wanted to be a *wife*. She had never wanted a *husband*. Both words were alien to her. She would have gone to her grave believing that she would never alter her thinking on the matter. Yet now she wanted him as her husband with a fervor that shook her to the core of her being. She would kill anyone who tried to take him from her.

"Liam," she said, her tone imperative.

He frowned. "Aye?"

"*This* is your time."

Liam held his breath and captured her gaze.

"*This* is your time," she stated again. "And I am your wife."

"Aye, that you are."

Silje's heart leapt at his calm assurance, at the steady light in his beautiful brown eyes. She had to be sure. "You will not be returning to the future?"

"Nay, I'm positive this was a one-way trip."

Silje scooted toward him a few inches, removed the leather tube and the used Christmas cracker from his hands, set them aside, and took his hands in hers. She squeezed them tight and he returned hers with a strong grip.

"What gives you this knowledge?"

"I...I can feel the truth in my...well...in my bones," he said, shrugging one shoulder. "These impressions are common in my family. They come from my Eire blood. I am here to stay."

Silje brought their hands to her chest. Their faces were only inches away from each other. She felt his breath on her cheek when he answered her next question.

"And what do your bones speak of now?"

"I'm home," he answered simply.

Silje's lips touched his and he pulled her into his arms so that she lay across his lap while his lips plundered hers.

Chapter Ten

Silje's senses whirled out of control. Liam's lips on hers teased and tasted, drew forth moans of pleasure. A raucous laugh from the men around the campfires reminded her they weren't alone.

She wrenched her lips away and clung to her husband. "They can hear us. They're laughing at me."

"Hush, now. They can't hear us over the sound of the fire and their own conversation." Liam stroked her hair back from her face and smiled down at her. "Why would they be laughing at you?"

"Because I never wanted a man." Her chest heaved and she held back tears of frustration and shame.

"They're jealous of me, I expect," Liam murmured. He nuzzled her neck. "I have a beautiful woman in my arms and they have to wait before they can hold their women."

"They can see our shadows on the tent walls," she gasped, arching toward him, tilting her head so she could feel more of his touch on her bare neck.

"That is easily solved," her husband said. He laid her on the bear-fur and blew out the candle. "There. We are in darkness except for the glow of the fires beyond."

Silje scooted backward on the sleeping bag so her whole body lay on the fur. The shadow of her husband knelt at her feet. He took one foot, removed her boot and sock, and slowly unwound the cloth binding the bottom of her trousers to her legs. She jerked her foot away as soon as it was bare. Liam picked up her other foot and repeated the process.

"You have beautifully formed feet," he mused. His warm hands massaged them and stroked her calves.

"My thanks," she squeaked. She hastily covered her mouth with her hand, stopping the groan of pleasure within.

Liam's hands left hers and she peered at him. He was

removing his boots, socks and winding cloths. He removed his belt and his cloak. Silje swallowed hard and steeled herself to act. She removed her own belt and her own cloak. The night air made her shiver yet her insides burned in unexpected anticipation.

When her husband's hands cupped her hips she had to stifle another groan. He used his chin to push aside the front opening of her jerkin. He pressed his cheek against her breast and she grabbed his shoulders.

"We're still wearing too much clothing," he whispered. His lips traced a path along her chin. "Do you agree?"

"Aye..."

One arm lifted her off the fur while the other removed her jerkin. He laid her down and then his strong hands pushed under her tunic and his flesh touched her bare flesh. She caught her breath at the wonder of it. She plucked at his tunic, wanting it gone. Liam knelt above her and whisked his tunic and under-tunic off. He cast them aside and pulled hers off too. The cold air struck her body and she gasped. Liam lowered himself over her and covered her with his warmth.

"Oh," she sighed, loving the feel of his chest pressing against her naked breasts.

"So soft," he whispered, slowly skimming his chest across hers. "So smooth."

Silje arched against him and caressed his bare flesh with her palms. She dug her fingers into his muscles and learned the shape of him. And then his lips were on hers and his tongue sought entrance. She opened her mouth and he swept in, tasting her, devouring her, spinning her desire into a woven cloth of longing and aching need.

Liam had never wanted a woman as much as he wanted Silje. His Norse wife. Her passion rose to meet his own even though he knew her to be a maiden. He had to go slow. He had to make this night good for her. He calmed his breathing and dragged his mouth from hers. He stroked the skin of her collar bone and felt her tremble. Liam rolled them onto her furs and

167

opened his sleeping bag. He flipped it, fur-side down, over top of them.

"Better?" he murmured.

"Aye," she panted.

Liam levered himself up onto one arm and cupped her breast in his hand. Her soft fullness fit perfectly in his palm and he rubbed the pad of his thumb across her pebbly nipple. Silje's breath caught in her throat in a most satisfying way.

"You're perfect," he groaned, burying his face in her neck.

"I...I am?" she whispered. Her fingers hesitated when they stroked the hairs on the back of his neck.

"Oh, aye." Liam moved his hand down and slipped it within the confines of her trousers so he could hold the warm flesh of her bottom. He used his grip to lift her hips against him. "Can you feel how much I want you? How much I long for you?"

"Liam," she breathed, moving her hips from side to side.

He groaned and kissed her. Her tongue warred with his in equal measure.

Soon. Soon, he thought.

And then...

"Our cold maiden is getting her own tonight! Is she not?"

The raucous shout caused Silje to stiffen. She tore her lips from his.

"Shut your mouth!"

"That was Audun. They're just here," Silje cried softly. "On the other side of the tent wall."

"Nay," Liam soothed, caressing her face. "They're still over by the fire."

"We should have moved the tent," she said, her body vibrating beneath him. "Away from the others. *Far* away."

"The poor man's got a fish in his bed. I feel sorry for the bastard."

Silje punched Liam's shoulder with the edge of her fist. "I will kill him. Let me up."

"Listen," Liam cautioned, turning his head. "I hear a scuffle. Someone is taking care of him for us."

They listened for five breaths before Audun spoke again.

"Throw him in his tent before Liam or Silje come out here and kill him. It would not be a great loss except we need him for the voyage home."

Further scuffling and grunts followed.

"Come, men. The other fires are just as warm. Let's leave the lovers in peace."

"I could kiss that man," Liam whispered, chuckling at the absurdity of the entire episode even as he shifted, uncomfortable due to his interrupted desires.

"I won't be able to show my face in the morning," Silje said, turning her head into the furs.

Damn. I've got to fix this.

Her husband took her head in his hands and turned it so she faced his shadow. He kissed her tight lips and she felt the smile in them.

"Do not laugh at me," she growled deep in her throat.

"Nay, luv. I smile because of how sorry I am for your father's men."

"How is this? How can you be sorry for them?"

"They are wretched men indeed because now they must try to find sleep with the thought of your retribution on their minds."

"You mock me?" she demanded, narrowing her eyes to slits. She pushed against his chest. "Get off."

Liam didn't move. Instead, he said, "You told me you were defiant."

"I am," she snapped.

"Then prove it. Ignore them and make love with me."

Silje tried to calm her angry breathing. She knew she was being unfair to Liam. It was not his fault that the cur had ridiculed her. Her husband wrapped his arms around her stiff body and then his legs around her hips and embraced her with all his strength. The air whooshed out of her chest and she struggled to take more than a shallow breath. His might was impressive and he would make a fine warrior once she trained him. Her pleasure in that expectation drained the rest of her resistance away.

"You are squeezing the life from me," she yelped in his ear.

Liam's arms immediately relaxed and she could breathe again. He pressed his cheek against hers.

"Silje. My Silje. Angry coupling can be fun, but that is not what I hoped for tonight."

She wriggled her arms free so she could lay a palm against his other cheek. "Is that what I am to you, Liam? Your Silje?"

"Aye," he whispered, even as his hands splayed across her bare back and tenderly pushed her against him. With each caress from her husband's hands passion flared. "And I am yours for I love you keenly."

"Love?" she whispered back, frowning, confused. Yet...yet his words struck at her heartstrings and brought a feeling of acceptance she had never known before. *Do I deserve this feeling?* "Love...love is not looked for in a...a Norse marriage."

"Is it not?" he asked in a wisp of sound next to her ear.

She shivered and squirmed against him. *What should I tell him? Should I tell him that I will kill anyone who tries to separate us? Is that love?* Silje wasn't certain.

"We have got to get rid of these trousers," he muttered next. His lips captured hers for a hard, thorough kiss. "Come, luv. Help me."

He sounded so desperate she had to stifle a giggle.

"Are you laughing at me now?" Liam's chuckle seemed strained. "I'm desperate with wanting you and you're laughing?"

"I am," she claimed boldly, drawing a proper laugh from her husband.

Their laughter dissolved once they lay fully naked beside each other. Liam's hand smoothed over her stomach and entered that region between her legs she'd thought to keep private. He cupped her there and exhaled across her breast. His hand moved on to stoke her inner thighs and she gasped, letting her legs fall open for him. Her being quivered in anticipation of his next touch. When it came she almost cried aloud.

"You are so soft. So beautiful."

His mouth opened over her nipple and he drew her into his mouth. Silje hadn't known that a man would suckle at a woman's breast. She had not known the sensation would be so incredible. When her husband moved between her legs she opened them wide and welcomed him. He positioned himself and slowly eased into her. Silje's eyes popped open and she heard her breath come in tiny pants.

"Are you all right? Silje?" Liam asked, pausing. He shook with the effort of controlling his movements.

"Do not stop," she begged, clutching at his shoulders.

"I won't. Easy does it," he whispered against her lips and drove forward smoothly. He covered her cry with his kiss.

Sharp pain startled her and then disappeared with his next careful thrust. Silje's breathing synchronized with every thrilling plunge. She wrapped her legs around him and ran her hands over his body. It seemed as though she couldn't touch enough of him. Her hips rose to meet his and Liam placed his head on her shoulder and groaned softly. She had not expected this pleasure. It built and built within her until she wanted to shout in frustration. Then, when she teetered at the edge, Liam ground into her and held her tight against him.

"Are you with me?" he begged.

"Always," Silje responded.

Liam circled his hips and pushed into her again. He grunted and spilled his seed. Ecstasy such as she'd never known erupted inside her. She arched her back and her husband held her tight as they rode the wave together, she with her hand over his mouth and he with his hand over hers, smothering the evidence of their union.

Liam held his wife close and tucked the bear-fur about them. He wondered if she was listening to the slowing beats of his heart. He rested his cheek against her head and sighed with contentment. Sleep tugged at him but he resisted, wanting to savor this moment. His heart was full—full of Silje—and he liked the feeling.

"Liam?"

"Aye?" he replied, stroking her naked shoulder.

"Why did you not ask if I loved you as well?"

Liam heard the hesitancy in her voice. *Is she afraid of my answer?* He lifted her chin and kissed her on the tip of her nose.

"You will declare yourself when you're ready. Love comes in its own good time."

Silje didn't respond immediately and he swallowed his disappointment. *Listen to your own counsel,* he admonished himself. *What did you expect? We've had hardly any time together. Just because you fell for her the moment you held her in your arms does not mean it was the same for her.*

"You are very confident," Silje finally whispered.

"I have reason to be."

"Why?"

Liam considered her question carefully and then answered in a quiet voice. "Because you did not want a husband and you did not want to be a wife. In spite of your strong opinion on the subject, we are married. I must be of great value to you otherwise you would have renounced me before your uncle. If you value me, you will one day love me. Soon I hope, but I am a patient man."

Silje stroked his chin and he turned his head and kissed her fingertips.

"Your reasoning is sound."

He grinned and pride swelled his chest. "I thought so."

"But your conclusion is flawed."

"Oh?"

Silje turned in his embrace until she could fold her arms on his chest and look down at him. He wished he could see her expression but the tent remained in shadow and all he could see was her outline. His stomach clenched and he held himself still, waiting for her explanation.

She kissed him tenderly and traced the line of his eyebrows. "Liam, my husband. I do not love you because I value you. I love you because you value *me*."

Liam's stomach unclenched. He gave a ragged laugh and hugged her close. "My sweet, sweet Silje."

His wife gave an indignant huff combined with a watery chuckle. It was an odd paring but it made sense when she murmured in a mock-stern tone, "I am not sweet. Everyone knows I am cantankerous. You will ruin my reputation with such talk."

Liam could not help a shout of laughter. She immediately shushed him. "Wife," he whispered as soon as he could speak, "we're going to have a wonderful, adventurous life!"

"Do you swear it, my good husband?"

"With all my heart."

Epilogue

At noon on the appointed day, Charlie parked on the side of the road as far onto the verge as he dared. He stepped on the emergency brake and waited. After three hours, he closed his book and heaved an anxious sigh.

"Damn it, Liam. Where are you?" he muttered, peering at the break in the trees where the barely-there path emptied out onto the verge.

The new year had brought six inches of snow. Not a lot by New Brunswick standards, but enough to make him worried about his friend. He refused to acknowledge that worry over snow was an excuse to ignore two weeks of continuous ominous impressions.

Charlie climbed out of his pick-up, locked it, and took his pack out of the back. He hefted it into place, closed the strap around his waist, pulled on his gloves and headed for the woods. He was going to look for Liam even though he knew deep in his soul that his friend would not—could not—be found. He tramped over the pristine snow and entered the woods.

"Not even a rabbit track," he said beneath his breath, looking down at the ground. "Bloody hell."

A little more than three hours later, Charlie reached Liam's campsite. The ground beneath the butternut tree was only dusted with snow. Silver food pouches lay strewn around the site, torn open by crows, he figured. He shook his head and searched the ground for further proof. When he found Liam's watch and compass, he pulled out his phone.

"9-1-1. Do you need police, fire, or ambulance?"

After explaining his situation, Charlie squatted against the butternut trunk, his arms resting on his knees, and waited for Ground Search and Rescue to arrive. He sighed and glanced around. He spied a folded shovel and, beside it, a rounded piece of iron in the dead grass. He picked up the piece of iron and turned it in his hands, brushing off bits of snow and rust. It was an iron boss. Liam had shown him a picture of one once. It came from the center of a Viking shield.

"Vikings," he said, passing a hand over his eyes, remembering the old witch at the fair.

Memories of that meeting had popped into his mind over and over again during the last two weeks. He'd even found himself looking for her in the street or at the mall. His obsession with her had become ridiculous. Charlie rested his head against the trunk and accepted the truth he'd felt while watching his friend hike into the woods.

Bloody hell. I'm never going to see Liam again.

Charlie sat there for a few minutes feeling sorry for himself. Then his jaw tightened and his teeth clenched. His slack hands curled into fists.

"Sod that," he growled softly. "I'm going to find you, old woman, and when I do, you're going to tell me where Liam is. Or *when* he is. Did you think I didn't notice that the only things left of my friend are modern? I'm not Biddy Early's descendant for nothing. Don't think you can hide from me."

Charlie's true intent, invisible but powerful, rippled out over the land as an explosion of power. It transcended time, space, and dimension. Like bumpers in a pinball machine, the ripple rebounded off of Earlys in every generation, gaining strength and focus, impossible to ignore.

* * *

In a cottage in the middle of somewhere, Aunty sat in a rocker, staring at the burning coals in the grate, holding Jeffry the guinea pig in her lap, petting him while he purred. Another successful Christmas had come to an end. There was nothing pressing to do now except prepare for the next one. A pile of seed catalogs sat at her elbow but there was still plenty of time to peruse those before winter's end. This year must be the year her Scarlet Runners would produce. She was convinced she'd been cursed by someone. Everyone else had success with the aggravating green beans.

"They're going to grow this year, blast them," she muttered.

Jeffry chirped.

Aunty's lips twitched. "Pessimist." And then she frowned and sat up straight. "Something's coming!"

Charlie's intent finally reached its target. The ripple had become a storm, a gale that buffeted her, tearing her white hair from its bun, whipping the strands about her face. Aunty raised a gnarled hand and waved it decisively. The power-filled wind abated. Tissue paper fluttered into place. Silk flowers floated back into terra cotta pots. Ribbons settled their dance and hung pensively from the rafters.

"Oh, dear."

The End

Dear Reader,

Here is a sneak peak at next year's Christmas Cracker Romance. I don't have a title yet, but the story will feature the S.S. Sicamous. You can find some information about this ship online: http://sssicamous.ca/history-of-the-sicamous/

Prologue

Aunty paced around her workshop while Jeffrey, the red and black brindle guinea pig, watched her from the corner of her bench. Her hands clenched and unclenched together behind her back.

"This isn't right, Jeffrey, it isn't," she muttered, shaking her hoary head, causing the loose bun of pure white hair to wobble about. "'Tis time to make another special Christmas cracker and I know he will be there—there where I will give it away."

Jeffrey chirped.

Aunty unclasped her hands and made a sweeping motion with one arm. "Nay, nay. The cracker is not for him. I must find a way to get the cracker to her without him catching me."

Jeffrey turned in a circle and chirped again.

Aunty stopped and stared at him, her arms akimbo, the light of the fire dancing around her, casting her face partially in shadow.

"Jeffrey, I have never heard you express such nonsense. Not do a special cracker this year? Not do a cracker?" she shook her head at him and turned aside.

Jeffrey purred as though in apology, drawing a short wave of one hand from his companion. Aunty drew her green, crocheted shawl closer about her and shuffled over to the diamond-paned windows. Snow fell and wind drifted it across her garden, thrusting the mass in triangular arcs up the stone walls surrounding the small cottage sitting in the middle of *somewhere*. The clear circle of the sun shone in an impotent circle through the clouds still heavy with unshed flakes.

Aunty growled softly. "There's been seven days of snow. An omen, that." She heaved a sigh. "Is it a good omen, or an ill? I do not know." The old woman shook herself and turned around with more energy. She pointed a finger at her guinea pig. "And don't you be asking if I know. 'Cause I don't."

Jeffrey blinked at her, appearing to choose to hold his own counsel.

"Regardless, there's a cracker to be made."

Aunty bustled around to the business side of her workbench, clapped her hands together, entwined her fingers and bent her combined hands out to crack her knuckles. Jeffrey chortled and hopped up and down.

"'Tis past time, you say? Aye, you've the right of it," she acknowledged.

Aunty plucked a sheet of pure red crepe paper from the dowels holding myriad colors next to the wall at her left. She smoothed the paper out before her on the bench and picked up her shears. Beneath her breath she hummed a familiar anthem while she cut out the large rectangle she needed to begin wrapping the cardboard tube at the center of the cracker and the two other rectangles required for the ruffled ends. At one point her hum turned into a poignant refrain, sung in her raspy, aged voice.

"*...and gentle maidens rise.*"

Then she picked up a glue stick and her singing subsided into humming again. Once the four-inch tube had been wrapped and the ruffles adorned with silver sprinkled borders, Aunty swiveled on her wooden stool and pulled the wooden box full of pre-cut wrapping paper toward her.

"I know exactly the one I want, I do," Aunty said, speaking to Jeffrey. "There's a white and red stripped beauty in here, I'm sure of it." She riffled through the colorful rectangles until she found the right one. Jeffrey bubbled and bobbed his head. "You like it? Me, too."

Jeffrey wheeked and Aunty smiled. "Aye, she'll be staying in Canada, where she's needed." Jeffrey wheeked again. "Aye." She stared suspiciously at her companion. "Are you trying to be funny?" The guinea pig chortled and Aunty snorted in reply. "Aye, you've the right of it. Some*when* else."

Aunty sobered, recalling the potential danger if *he* showed up and stopped her from giving the special cracker away.

Charlie. Charlie Early. That was his name. She would not say it aloud in case by its utterance she drew his attention to her. He was looking for his friend, Liam, and Charlie would not give in until he found him. Liam could not be found…not in this time, anyway. Charlie's search was futile, but his determination and his lineage made him a powerful challenger.

Aunty remembered Biddy Early—Bridget Ellen Early. She had been a strong-minded woman with a powerful influence over the lives of those who came to her for help. If Charlie Early was related to her, and Aunty felt in her bones that he was, he might have reserves of power that could disrupt her own calling. *I will not permit it*, she thought.

Aunty set the glue-gun aside, collected any stray threads of glue, and held the decorated tube before her. Pleased with the white ribbon spirals and the tiny felt red apples, she reached for a ruffle and closed one end of the cracker in preparation for filling it, making certain the snap stayed firmly in place, all while she chanted in a low, throbbing voice. One by one she dropped the prizes, the motto, the hat, and the sweet into the empty tube. Next she pinched the open end closed, attached the ruffle, and set the special Christmas cracker in the carved wooden box built to hold it.

She stood for the last part of the spell, reaching high in the air, her fingers spread, drawing the energy she needed from the world around her, ordering it, and then channeling it into the Christmas cracker. The swirling eddies of air calmed, the dancing ribbons hung straight, and the roaring fire died to a comfortable blaze. Jeffry chirped as his long hair settled back into place.

"There," she panted, closing the hinged lid. "That will do."